THE FUTURE IS SHORT

VOLUME 3

Top 10 Finisher

Best
Print/Electronic
Book Publisher

PREDITORS & EDITORS
READERS' POLL 2016

BOOKS FROM LILLICAT PUBLISHERS

VISIONS SERIES

THE FUTURE IS SHORT

SCIENCE FICTION IN A FLASH

VOLUME 3

Editors

S. M. Kraftchak

Paula Friedman

J. J. Alleson

Emily Johnson

LILLICAT PUBLISHERS
USA

THE FUTURE IS SHORT, VOLUME 3

POD ISBN: 978-1-945646-10-2
EPUB ISBN: 978-1-945646-11-9
MOBI ISBN: 978-1-945646-12-6

CONTENTS

INTRODUCTION

Life is more than a dream, but that's how it begins. In utero, our brain forms and sparks to life. Random firing of synapses that organize currents and chemicals into logical and artistic purpose. It is this blend of cause that drives our goals. Made of the same material, we infinitely divide to define our own device of form and function. In the Science Fiction Microstory Contest, ingenious authors from around the world unite each month on a theme, but the stories they produce couldn't be more different.

From the mention of a single word, Flight, your thoughts expand to envision a large commercial aircraft, the soaring of a beautiful winged creature, the buzzing of a tiny insect, or perhaps an action to escape the walls we build around ourselves. Break from those chains of reality and step into the world of science fiction, where anything is possible.

Signs shroud the landscape to determine our path as a shepherd might herd sheep, but metaphorically, the word could be but a clue of that to come or a symbol within an alien language. In this vast universe, Monsters of distant worlds are already communicating their designs upon other such herds that have failed to hear their message. Or perhaps we are that herd?

Stories can predict these futures that expand in front of us as lines on a sheet. Those drawn form into Memory, are organized deep within our minds when we sleep, and act as the catalyst of our dreams. But, which came first, the dream or the thought? I would say the prior.

We are all merely dreamers from birth.

Jot Russell
Science Fiction Microstory Contest Creator
Science Fiction Microstory Contest Group Founder

FLIGHT

January 2016

Winner
"Flight"
S. M. Kraftchak

FLIGHT

S. M. Kraftchak

Can Ayalyn prove she's not who authorities claim she is?

Ayalyn squeaked as she flew from her captor's hands, and thudded to the floor. Instantly, she snatched the blindfold from her eyes, scrambled to her feet, and rushed the door. She jumped back as the door dropped into place with a thunk. "It wasn't me." She tipped her head up to look into the security camera. "I don't belong here. I'm not one of them."

A pleasant woman's voice sounded. "You have been detained in the Hawksbill Space Eyrie. You will remain here until your trial. Your estimated wait time is four hundred thirty-two Terran cycles. Hawksbill is a full-service detention facility. We hope your stay is comfortable."

Barely holding her tears at bay, Ayalyn turned to examine the ten-foot round sphere. The floor, only three-feet wide from side to side, gave access to the barest amenities: a retractable hammock; a bidet; a stainless steel sink the size of her open hand; and a table next to the hammock. A tablet, imbedded in the table, and a single potted daisy were the only tools provided to maintain her sanity in the days to come. She frowned at the narrow beam of sunlight shooting through the four-inch window onto her feet, clenched her fists and screamed in fury. A moment later her body arched and her back began the now familiar cramping, followed by shooting pain from her hips to her shoulders. Dropping to her hands and knees, she panted as she waited for the pain to subside.

The pleasant woman suddenly spoke. "Your distress has been noted. Assistance will be dispatched within twelve hours. Residents wishing a more immediate resolution to their distress need only push the large green button next to the door."

Breathing heavily, Ayalyn looked over her shoulder and crawled toward the button, stood on her knees to press it, but suddenly collapsed into a fetal position as another vicious spasm wracked her back and rendered her unconscious.

When she opened her eyes, the shaft of sunlight shone on the opposite side of the sphere. Her whole body ached and her back was on fire, even laying still. Without sitting up, she realized a tray of food had been slid onto her table and a pungent sour smell filled the space. Pinching her nose and breathing through her mouth, she slowly got to her feet and turned away from the tray when her stomach threatened to revolt. She burst into tears and wailed, "Help me."

"Assistance has been dispatched and will arrive in six hours. If residents wish more immediate assistance, they may press the green button next to the door."

Ayalyn didn't hesitate and launched herself at the green button. Instantly the door slid into the sphere above her. In the sudden decompression, she managed to throw herself to the floor as the potted flower and tray of putrid food tumbled past her. The smooth floor afforded her hands no purchase as her feet slid into space. Squealing in panic, she slammed her hands onto the sides of the door. Gasping for breath, Ayalyn glanced over her shoulder at the five-thousand-foot drop and nearly let go as fear weakened her grip. "Help me! Now!"

"Residents choosing more immediate assistance need no further—"

Ayalyn's hands suddenly slipped from the frame and she fell backward into empty air. With her arms frozen in their last desperate reach, she watched her sphere and dozens more bobbing in the air, recede as she fell. Trembling with fear as her body tipped over so she faced her approaching fatal end, Ayalyn's back suddenly cramped and arched. A heartbeat later, her body jerked backward as a pair of leathery gray wings extended and filled with air, arresting her fall. Wide-eyed with amazement, she instinctively flexed her wings, soared up past her former sphere, and burst into laughter. "I guess I am one of them."

Whether voyaging the universe or journeying in a fantasy world of her own making, S.M. Kraftchak is passionate about discovering unique characters and relentlessly tracing their heartfelt stories so she can relate them to her readers. She loves sunrise on the beach, sunset in the mountains, and portraying Elizabeth Tudor. She has one dog who pretends to be a footrest, another who almost catches a Frisbee, and a cat who trades desk space for open-window-time. S.M. has three awesome daughters and a husband who is her best friend, her harshest critic, and her most fervent supporter. www.smkraftchak.com

Recon

W.A. Fix

A crack Galactic Recon Team is overwhelmed by a single invisible enemy on a primitive world.

The dart passed within six inches of Decker's right ear. The hiss of its black and yellow flights startled him, but it was well by before he could react. It struck Collins high on the right shoulder with a slight pop.

"Oww damn it!" yelped Collins, as he instinctively pulled the thing out and looked at it. "Where the hell . . .?" he said as he turned glaring at Decker. . . .

Decker didn't have time to say anything before Collins dropped the dart, staggered slightly then dropped to his knees. Within seconds his eyes glazed, then he fell face first onto the Jungle floor.

"Command, this is Recon One. Collins is down. I repeat: Collins is down," Decker said into his com set.

"Down? From what? You just broke the tree line three minutes ago," said mission commander Burntz.

"Sir, he got hit with a dart and was down before we knew what happened," said Decker.

Decker looked up from Collins' body just in time to see Phillips fall to the ground with another black and yellow flighted dart stuck in his back. Within five seconds Jacobs yelled and pawed at an identical dart in his left buttock. Seconds later he joined Collins and Phillips.

"Everybody down and cover!" yelled Decker as he dove for cover behind the nearest tree.

"Command, Phillips and Jacobs are also down. Do you have vitals? I see no movement," said Decker.

"This is Command, vital monitors are flat line. How many colors are the flights on those darts?"

"All the same. Each has four fins, two black, two yellow, alternating." said Decker.

"Recon One, they color code the flights. You have one hostile. Collect one of those darts and get your ass back to base. Do not touch it with your bare hands, we have no idea what poison it contains."

"One hostile! Are you serious? One primitive on this backwater planet just took out three Galactic Fleet Recon team members. Are you shittin' me? . . . Boss, we need to leave these people alone," said Decker.

He opened his sample case, pulled out a specimen box and needle-nose pliers. Collins lay four feet away and the dart was within reach between them. He casually snatched up the dart with the pliers and dropped it into the box. He stored the box inside his vest then said, "Control, I have the sample. We need a location for the hostile."

"Recon One, we have a small heat signature fifteen meters to your southeast. Nothing else within fifty meters on motion, IR or UV."

"Everyone, get ready for suppression fire to the southeast!" yelled Decker to the remaining four team members. He heard the team readying their weapons. "Saddle up! We are moving back to base in standard retreat formation. Mason, you are on me. Wilson, you have Shaw and Harris. As soon as we hit the tree line break formation and haul ass, base will cover our retreat from there . . . Ready? . . . Move out!"

Mason and Decker began firing full automatic. The electro-magnetic weapons erupted in fire, sending bursts of fifty projectiles at nearly a kilometer per second. When he heard the firing begin behind him he turned and ran through the firing line. As he passed Wilson, the man dropped to the ground, a dart standing like a dandelion from his neck. He and Wilson stopped at the tree line, turned and began firing. Within seconds Shaw and Harris passed them at full speed, breaking into the open.

"Go!" he yelled to Mason, giving him two seconds then he turned and ran. Cover fire was coming from the compound as he and Mason went through the gate.

Breathing heavily, he turned back to the jungle and suddenly felt a dart pierce his right bicep.

Shocked, Decker took two steps backward, then realized he couldn't feel his right arm. A heavy fog began to obscure his vision. He was confused, and somehow the ground hit him in the face.

W.A. Fix is a retired Information Technology Professional, who, with his wife and three cats, lives in the suburbs of San Diego, California. He is passionate about life, the everlasting beauty of the earth, and the survival of the creatures that live there. He has written fiction all his life and within the last few years realized that writing helps him see the world more clearly. Several of his works are published throughout the web and he is a featured author in numerous anthologies of flash fiction and longer short stories. Search for his author page on Amazon.com.

INTO THE DARK

Paula Friedman

. . . for they must find a crack wherein to hide

It was not safe in the air anymore. It was not safe on the ground. *Where now*, asked the matriarch, *to seek cool darkness? Where anymore to take flight?*

For there was nothing, nowhere. This barren Earth only. For three centuries, they had written of these days, back in those times when writing yet was possible and speech moved even across far distances that now took long cycles of years to trek. "Come, Ritan, Tisa, Moro," called the matriarch; the children gathered close beneath her umbra. "Let us march beyond the rocks until the Light." For they must, by Light-rise, find a crack wherein to hide.

Two cycles back, an ancient find—a "hous," as the scholarly old slab-comber called it—had provided shelter through the hottest half-year, not even cracking at high noon. They had lived gently through those months; little Lena, pregnant by Moro, had even given birth ("To twins!" the young had exclaimed, until the matriarch had seen needful to ease the smaller sib from its mother's arms, for no sooner had it birthed than died). That spring had come softly, gently—a good year in the centuries of heated dearth and dryness, boiling equatorial plains, drained lost riverine. Even, there'd been brief weeks of small marigolds and, down a dell between two boulders in a shaded slip, one blue-streaked violet, and the new baby's chirping cries. A beautiful season, two seasons, of hope.

They had found time, then, to seek new caches of the ancient foods, to grow a tiny stock of grainy plants from the last bagged seeds. And time to build—clay spread by lank Ritan, with newly fresh creative eyes, in swirled vital patterns (always with the Earth prayer but in lively ways!)—building, in the old hous shade, new mound-homes. "Our glory, our glorious hope!" laughed Moro, the man always silent except when he sang love to Lena and their babe. The matriarch drew her umbra-robe, her shader, high and nodded, echoed in this movement by the other adults, "Hope, yes. May we, Earth's children, stay alive."

For there were no others, not in human form, anymore. Thus, burdened by each other's odors, unhappily Ritan and Tisa humped. The matriarch looked on. "And multiply," she prayed. Yet not to become too many—no, never again; should this gift-season be a chance, it must be chance that never again might lead to this.

Springlike hours of that night, and then a morning and a single bird's song in the afternoon gave way through one more night into a glistening dawn, and summer came, and Hot-light. Two dawns later, the ancient marbled "roof" twanged; even as the Evening Star arose, the last-standing ancient hous cracked, crumbled crashing, and collapsed.

Columns about them; rocks fell down.

The clay homes underneath were crushed, the babe and Moro gone, Lena so blood-drained she could not survive. Tisa, too, was injured, Ritan dragging her along. The old scholar limping after. These last few children of the folk of Earth.

Heavily, again the matriarch led them in the endless flight, seeking another crack, another brief-survival's huddling-place, a temporary shielding from the Light.

Yet nowhere to flee. No sheltering sky or land. Only one single mound, one lone broken-off survival of the times before appeared: "They call this gah-rage," the scholar croaked. Tiny it was, too, built of long-crumbled bricks. And in it, a metal object under a large slate: "Shovey," the scholar pointed. Ritan raised its wooden end. "Shovey—to push."

Night after night they dug, digging and pushing with Shovey, for shelter from the blistering Light. Under the stars, each weakly shoved and dug to break a hole to deep-delve shelter, for, far far below, some soil must yet be cool.

14

Until, knew the matriarch, *the heating catches up. And our bodies ever weakened, and the handle of the long-dried shovey ever cracking so we must stop to seek out a shrunken vine to mend it with, and with our souls, too, faltering—*

Dark succeeded light, light dark. Overhead the last condor spiraled, watchful, until it too, dried, fell from flight.

Paula Friedman is the author of The Rescuer's Path, called "exciting, physically vivid, and romantic" by Ursula Le Guin, "Lyrically written" by Small Press Review, and "Vivid, humane, and wise" by Cheryl Strayed. Friedman's award-winning short fiction and poetry appeared in over forty journals and anthologies. A professional editor, Friedman served as lead manuscript editor for TFIS volume 1. Her website is paula-friedman.com. Her new novel of the late-1960s Berkeley antiwar movement is scheduled for 2017 publication. www.paula-friedman.com

NOTHING BUT FLOWERS

Andrew Gurcak

Fun language fact: the collective noun for quadrillions of blossoms is invasion.

The skies blossomed in regimented profusion.

Specks in the tens of quadrillions arrayed themselves with geometric precision high above every point on the earth. At first they may have seemed to drift dreamily through atmospheric layers, but no storm or jetstream could even briefly nudge them from the verticality of their descent. Scarcely more than dust motes, visible from below only by their sheer numbers as a brightness sparkling through the air, they neither deviated nor swerved from their straight-line descent, exhibiting a determination bespeaking an impossible obstinacy. Whatever guided them, whatever physics they recognized as lawful, was constrained to one direction only: down. If they were stopped above the ground by encountering an object, they would permit the object to slide through them, raising themselves if needed, then immediately move to settle still closer to the ground. Their initial descent stopped a few feet above whatever—building, ocean, ground—lay directly beneath them, where they hovered, having shaped themselves into a perfect coating.

The motes then bloomed: leisured fireworks unfolding into nacreous squares. Their blossoming took them down to the last fraction of an inch of their descent. They joined together, were now seamless and one. In the air, through the waters, there was a release of unearthly molecules that gave every living creature the surety that whatever their species craved most basically was at hand, surely to be theirs. For the majority of creatures, it was certainty that predators were absent, food was present, it was time to mate. For humans, it could be that wealth was theirs, that true love was before them, that whatever faith they had followed was judged by their god to be well-performed, and that now was the moment of their reward for doing so.

After a moment in the experience of such bliss, every person experienced a voice:

We are the covering. We are the prompt tools of evolution. We know you. We see here the smallest step beyond a beginning. You are incipience, and to grow you, we will shape the balance of organisms here to safeguard proper growth. We are come to make the progress certain. Evolution has led your world to useful pathways, but, being clumsily random, the evolution as it exists here has taken you also to byways, even dead-ends. Consciousness in animals, that you so acclaim, is a dead end. The existence of animals itself constitutes an intolerable hindrance. The obviousness of that fact will become evident to you.

For you as animals, you hold a pinnacle of evolution to be the ability to move, and so you have become adept at it: believing that ways to move more quickly, more adroitly are achievements. There is, however, another physics, as you would term it, that is equally valid and, based on our own experience and evolution, more useful. We have contemplated and advanced what a being can do with limited or, better, no motion. We direct ourselves not to deviate, never to swerve. And yet we progress, as we have now demonstrated to you. We gift you our physics.

The one capability required for elements of your biosphere to enter the living universe is the ability to absorb directly the energies of your sun, and from that evolve into beings that can utilize every energy hierarchy of the cosmos. What some of your constituents demonstrated as a first step, photosynthesis, is essential, though rudimentary. Those organisms that now possess that ability are those that must develop unencumbered, free of obstructions that your existence represents. We are here to assist them.

There can no more be animals. There is no gain by delay, so we will perform that task expeditiously. We are not cruel, and will gift you the kindness of one day. Use it to ponder and learn, and, in the fashion you choose, prepare yourselves for your end. We have given you the gift of complete happiness as you understand it. With that understanding will come acceptance and gratitude that your end serves a much greater purpose than your existence ever could.

All were indeed calm. They looked on impending death with equanimity. No fears ensued, no anxieties intruded on their endings.

One day passed. All animal life went extinct.

The petal covering released further gases that sped the decomposition of all that was not plant-like. The covering itself then dissolved into a nourishment that compressed millions of years of evolution into the planned perfection of direct energy absorption.

Plants flourished.

Andy Gurcak is retired. He and Elaine divide their time between their home in Pittsburgh and a cottage in the Finger Lakes region of upstate New York. A great many of their most satisfying times are the experiences shared with their three young grandchildren.

FLIGHT OF THE BUICK

Gary Hanson

A story of space age advertising attraction.

Ted Dodger was driving along County Road VV just a little outside of Somerset; although he had been drinking earlier at the Cajon Club (the last of the strip clubs in western Wisconsin) he did not feel particularly impaired. The road conditions were fair for mid-January, with a light dusting of snow, and although he was pushing his Buick LaCrosse well beyond the posted speed limit, he was still surprised when the accident occurred. The local police received a dispatch from the Buick's OnStar of an accident and found Ted sitting at the side of the road, dazed, but like many drunks he came out of the accident without any major injuries.

"Mr. Dodger, can you tell me what happened here?" asked Officer Campbell.

"I'm not sure, I think I was in an explosion. I remember trying to avoid hitting a deer, then the road blew up around me. The next thing I remember was sitting up in the snow," said Ted.

"Were you alone in the car?" asked Officer Campbell.

"Yes," said Ted.

Officer Campbell, finding Ted confused and smelling of alcohol, back tracked the path Ted left in the snow up a nearby hill to the base of a billboard for the Allen's Flower Shop in New Richmond, which had been almost totally obliterated. However, other than some small debris Officer Campbell could find no trace of the Buick or any tire tracks leading to or away from the hillside. After taking several pictures of the scene, Officer Campbell took Ted back east to where Ted had indicated he last remembered driving. It being early Sunday morning, the only tracks along the road appeared to be from the Buick. When cresting a hill, they came to a section of road where the car tracks suddenly stopped in a large area that appeared to be blown clear of all snow. Getting out of his squad car Officer Campbell walked up the road, noticing that sections of the road were missing and the area off to the west appeared to form a slight mound of loose dirt. After taking some more photos of the area and making notes for his report, Officer Campbell returned to his squad car, calling the police dispatcher and asking them to have the county highway department to come out to the scene and post warning signs until the road could be repaired.

About 3 hours later outside of San Diego, California, a meteor flashed through the sky. At the impact scene, the local authorities found a melted mass which had a Wisconsin license plate belonging to a Buick LaCrosse, registered to a Mr. Ted Dodger, and a section of billboard with a picture of white poinsettias. The local police proclaimed it a hoax.

Interestingly, during the DWI and insurance fraud trials of Mr. Dodger, evidence is presented showing definitive proof that OnStar and ESA space radar tracked an object from Wisconsin to an impact in California. Scientist are then able to determine from the orbital path that the object mass is the size of a two-mile-wide asteroid, but since California could not have survived an impact with anything of that size, it must have been something else. Over the years that follow, using this original data, the orbit of the mysterious object is confirmed to have been a dark matter asteroid. Dark matter is made up of special material that, although it has gravity, does not interact with normal matter; thereby it is forced to orbit through the earth but never impact with it. The Buick, due to its course, speed, and size happened to match the elongated dark matter asteroid enough that the gravity captured each other until the dark matter asteroid intersected with the ground again in California. Mr. Meyer was indeed fortunate that the impact with the billboard threw him clear of the Buick before it was dragged into deep space.

Of course, some advertising executive created a commercial coining the saying "Flight of the Buick - Even dark matter cannot resist the attraction of the LaCrosse."

Gary Hanson is an inventor and entrepreneur; having worked for 20 years for a Fortune 100 company before starting his own new product design company, specializing in automated equipment for the wholesale bakery industry. While an inveterate reader and lover of science fiction and graphic novels, Gary has written for trade journals, filed several per-se patents, and dreams about the future realities of science concepts in today's news. He strongly believes in Sci-Fi stories based on hard science, with unexpected plot line twists.
Gary lives near Somerset, a small town in west-central Wisconsin.

FIRST FLIGHT

Jon Ricson

A music graduate assistant travels through time with his Professor to witness a classical music treasure, and a royal assassination.

We had come forward to see *The Tale of Tsar Saltan,* an opera by Nikolai Rimsky-Korsakov. (And by come *forward,* dear reader, I mean we had walked through a doorway in the basement of a Chicago college building in 1891, and found ourselves standing outside the Kiev Opera House in 1911. We did not seem to "appear" as much as just *be* there. No one seemed to notice us as anything but regular folk of 1911 attending an opera.)

Not until we had handed our tickets to the usher and had been seated was I able to regain my composure, as this was my first travel through time.

As the Professor had related to me prior, this opera of Rimsky-Korsakov featured an overture called "The Flight of the Bumblebee". He had spoken about it with such reverence that I was intrigued to hear it.

As if the evening were not exciting enough, I noticed many armed guards about. Minutes before the curtain rose, I found the answer for their presence as the Russian Tsar was announced and everyone stood in respect. The Professor winked at me and clapped vigorously with the rest of the crowd.

Not long after the first act was under way, I noticed the Professor taking careful glances at the royal upper boxes. He carefully opened and held close his cigarette case, which of course was not a cigarette case at all. He read something on the strange surface inside. (I still had not become clear on the design of this peculiar device he used so frequently. But I knew that he could do any number of things with it, including note taking, viewing still, or even small moving images, and—more shockingly —hearing music and sound much better than a phonograph!)

To disguise his actions, he retrieved a dummy cigarette from the case which he did not light, nor bother to put to his lips. The Professor had many vices, but smoking was not one of them. He then returned the case to his coat pocket.

The overture began after the first scene of the third act. An actor was turned into a bumblebee for some plot device, and the piece started. I was amazed at the virtuosity it took to facilitate the notes involved. Notes literally flew faster than I thought possible.

Once the relatively short piece ended, the trouble started.

Madness erupted above in the royal alcoves. Guards began moving about, looking upwards at the Tsar's box. A gun shot rang out! Then another!

The Professor tugged at my coat and nodded towards a quiet exit, away from the melee happening around the royal contingent. I followed the Professor as he kept a quick pace to the door. The orchestra began to play a vaguely familiar tune.

I crinkled my nose. "Is that God Save the Tsar?"

He looked back, nodded and smiled.

Once we were away from the Opera House, we slowed as more soldiers and police passed us on the way to the wild scene we had left blocks behind.

We sat at a local outdoor café, which had closed for the evening, to catch our breath.

"So the tickets we used, *they* are what brought us through the doorway to this time and place?" I was still quite new to this process. He nodded and looked again at his cigarette box.

"I procured them in auction . . . some time . . . hence," he said and sniffed. I presumed he meant in the future.

"So the Tsar . . .?" I asked.

"The Tsar will be fine," he smiled, reading his device. "The Prime Minister . . . will not be as lucky."

"So you knew the outcome, the trouble that would erupt, yet still we came?" I asked.

"When I found these tickets, I thought it would be interesting to attend and hear *The Flight of the Bumblebee*. It's always been one of my favorites. I also thought this would be a good *first flight* for you as well, so you can see the educational, anthropological, and historical possibilities these kinds of journeys hold."

I had been his graduate assistant for most of the scmcster, but when he had shared how he had come upon his various pictures and mementos throughout music history I had been dubious. But now, there was no doubt. We had actually traveled through time and space!

This would be just the first of my many strange and astonishing adventures with The Musicologist.

Jon Ricson is a speculative fiction writer and has been published in online magazines, science fiction anthologies, and in many monthly writing contests. He resides outside Orlando, Florida and you can often find him strolling the streets of Disney thinking creative thoughts. He is finally finishing his first full sci-fi novel with plans to seek publishing. Find out more about Jon at http://www.JonRicson.com.

PROPHECY

February 2016

Winner
"Feedback"
Andrew Gurcak

FEEDBACK

Andrew Gurcak

We're omnipresent, and we're here to help you.

Good morning, David. Be seated. We have required your physical presence here at the behest of your potential employer. Since this is your first session using iProphesy, please focus on the green dot in the center of the screen. Do not blink for two seconds. Now, state your full name, then certify that you have read and agreed to our Terms and Conditions. We apologize for the fuss, but both you and we want to keep our lawyers happily ensconced in their holding pens. If at any time you wish to speak to a human, say, "Human, please", and we'll connect you with our next available human Human Interaction Specialist.

With your implied permission, we have gathered your academic, financial, genetic, medical, and previous employment data; all public surveillance, photographic and sensor data; all social media metadata; all data from your parents' home and your college dormitories' sensor systems; and all audio-video datastreams from dwellings you have lived in since college. We have further accessed all first-level contact data from every person you have met since the age of six. We analyzed these against the trillions of other personal data we have in our possession, and may have supplemented them from sources we are not at liberty to disclose. In compliance with the Fair Isaiah Act, we are pleased to share with you the following synopsis of our findings:

At 24 years old, you appear to be in good overall health. There are, however, anomalies present in your genome. You have a pre-disposition to certain cancers that may become malignant in later decades, but, taking into account projected improvements in health care, none appear to suggest imminent or long-term danger to you. We have numerous data of your indulging excessively in alcoholic beverages and both licit and illicit drugs that go beyond occasional recreation, and the records of your cars' sensors show that you are quite willing to drive at excessive speed, both relative to road and weather conditions, and in absolute terms. We have similarly noted your repeated attempts to override your vehicles' autonomous systems, significant both because you clearly desired to drive in a manner that would showcase your sense of rebelliousness, and because you refuse to acknowledge the demonstrated futility of your actions despite consistent failures. As such, we believe that you have a significant probability of being involved in a serious, possibly fatal, vehicular accident in the next five years.

We have seen, as the above would indicate, repeated incidents of excessive thrill-seeking on your part. This goes well beyond that normatively exhibited by adolescents and young adults. We project that you will continue to engage in numerous casual sexual encounters, but that you will eventually marry eleven years from now. You will likely seek a woman similar to you in terms of propensity for thrill-seeking, and you will marry based on a short, likely whirlwind, period of courtship. Given the personalities of both of you, we project that you both will initiate extensive affairs outside your marriage, and that you will divorce three years after your marriage date. The presence of unplanned children may complicate the exact timing of these estimates.

Your attainment of less-than-average grades will, as you are now doubtless aware, put you in substantial difficulty in maintaining employment long-term, given the trends we are forecasting in human jobs availability. You do possess resources and skills ("good looks", "charm") for human-human interactions and again, based on our datasets, we project that you will be able to maintain an average-low lifestyle, at least for the next several decades of the world economy.

You may ask what you can do to change the probabilities that the precipitating events will occur, and/or their likely outcomes. You may object that, unlike a statue or figurine, you have the capability to change what you are and significantly modify your behavior. We applaud such initiatives on your part, but based on our latest recursive feedback algorithms, we project that modification is unlikely (< 2%) to last for an extended period of time, much less be in any sense permanent. But, as we always say, only YOU can generate your Bayesian priors, and despite our ever-expanding training datasets, we may occasionally err in our extrapolations. Our corporate motto, after all, is "Correlation, Not Causation".

On behalf of the iProphesy team, intellagents and humans alike, we appreciate this opportunity to serve you. Please remain seated to complete our mandatory customer satisfaction survey.

Thank you, and have a pleasant afternoon.

Andy Gurcak is retired. He and Elaine divide their time between their home in Pittsburgh and a cottage in the Finger Lakes region of upstate New York. A great many of their most satisfying times are the experiences shared with their three young grandchildren.

EINSTEIN'S HEAD

Kalifer Deil

This little tale leads to a quantum disaster of untold proportions.

I had this small bust of a cross-eyed Einstein above my desk at the Institute with the inscription "Spooky Actions at a Distance" on the base. This was one of many of his quotes concerning his doubts about quantum mechanics. I took it as a prophecy that we would find nature to be deterministic. Of course, things have not gone the way Einstein would have liked.

To show my determinism, I made my own Institute business cards, with a picture of a gear and a wrench on it that states "Hillman Bentley / Quantum Mechanic." Okay, I'm regarded as a bit eccentric, but having a name composed of two extinct cars certainly adds to that image.

I just finished my active panel presentation in house showing that quantum entanglement relies on three more dimensions, in addition to the 11 dimensions of M-Theory. When particles are entangled, I showed they share a common point in this quantum space. This is all a big mathematical exercise so no one here really believes the results. My iPad 12.0 stylus pen didn't work on the active wall pancl so I uscd my finger; not impressive. A few months back, I called it God's space to Dieter, a colleague, and he got red-faced and shouted something back at me in unintelligible German.

This group, before me, was silent until a man in the back of the hall raised his hand to start the Q and A session. The tall man rose and stated, "I'm Keith Kantrowitz from MIT. Why do you think this space exists?"

I shot back, "Why do you think the three dimensions we seem to occupy exists?"

"Well, we are here to witness it. Who is witnessing your quantum space?"

I paused to think of an answer. "You can see from the equations that we cannot see what is going on in quantum space. However, someone or something in quantum space can see us and affect us. I think that's quite remarkable."

"Are you implying God lives there?"

"God? No! Well, not quite. It does mean that we could be a simulation in quantum space but not the other way around, but I'm not really suggesting that."

There were no further questions so I went back to my office rather dejected, only to see Dieter at my door.

"Coming to gloat over my demise, Dieter?"

"No, no. I've been studying your equations since last spring. I've built this device that I think can break the very tenuous bonds between our space and this quantum space assuming your equations are correct. I thought you might want to witness a first test."

I raised an eyebrow, "It should just break entanglement. Dennis Hsu has a QM communication experiment set up. He was at the talk so he probably went back to his lab. This should disrupt it so let's go."

Dr. Hsu's lab door was open. "Dennis, is your experiment running now?"

"Yes. Why?"

"Do you mind if we try to disrupt it with Dieter's device? He thinks it will break entanglement. It has about a 5-degree cone of directionality, so point to where to aim it."

"Well, practically anything breaks entanglement so I won't be too impressed; but sure, go ahead right where I'm pointing." Dieter aimed it carefully and flipped the switch.

"Jesus! Turn it off!" I shouted. The clap of air rushing to fill a vacuum was so loud I could barely hear anything except the ringing in my ears. Dr. Hsu had blood spurting from the remaining stub of his index finger. A maw gaped in the experimental apparatus, the table, the floor, and the sub-basement floor, on into darkness. "Dieter, you've just made matter non-exist!"

Dr. Hsu, gripping his finger to stop the bleeding, said, "Dieter, whatever that is, it's more dangerous than any nuke!"

Dieter, wide eyed, said, "I'm afraid Hillman's cat is out of the box. I posted the schematics on the Web this morning. Any teen could make it in an hour!"

Dieter rushed to his office to delete the information from the Web. I rushed to my office to send out a memo to destroy all copies. I looked out my office window later that day and could see whole buildings disappearing, followed by claps of thunder. Dieter was right; teens were onto this and it was spreading.

I muttered sadly to myself, "Simulation Over?"

Kalifer Deil is the pseudonym for Gary Feierbach, a Silicon Valley engineer and computer scientist. He writes mostly hard science fiction for fun and to exercise his imagination. He has written the Tillian 5 trilogy, The Diary of Professor Gilbert Rasher and many other novellas and short stories. His website, http://www.kaliferdeil.com, contains many interesting articles and stories. He is currently working on a novel called Jane.

PARADOX PROPHESY

Gary Hanson

*You can travel into the past to a fixed point
but only if someone tells you which point that was.*

Gerald JoAnson looked up from his computer as the test object vanished into the time vortex. Once again, the object bounced back off the incident horizon and came instantly flying back out of the vortex, dissolving like a ghost image of itself. "Dammit, what are we doing wrong? The math says that this should work!"

"We must be misinterpreting the math. There is a conservation principle at work, it only works for conditions where it already worked," said Matt.

'Hmm,' thought Gerald. 'That might be the problem. We aren't just sending back an object, but a section of space-time, forming an infinite causality loop of increasing space-time projecting to the future.

"What do you suggest we do?" asked Matt.

Banias Dig Site: (in Biblical times called Caesarea Philippi)

Henry Johanson looked up from the dig site in the Grotto of Pan. The cave was cool, a welcome relief from the temperatures outside. Even this high in the Golan Heights, the August temperature was oppressive for the Minnesota native- upper nineties in the shade. Henry was mucking out the hole at the back of the spring when he found a miniature statue. He noticed it appeared to be Roman and still sealed. Getting his camera, he went back to the spot he had been digging and, placing a context tag marker, took a number of photos, and made an entry in his notebook. Then, placing it in a Ziploc bag, he carefully carried it out to Professor Ramstad's tent.

"Professor, look what I just found," called Henry.

After looking at it through the plastic, they carried it to a sink and opened the bag. Setting the statue on a paper towel, the professor carefully took a squirt bottle of water, a pen needle probe, and a worn toothbrush and started cleaning the surface. After a little while, being satisfied that the relic was fairly sturdy and that the mud was not the only thing holding the object together, the professor cleared the mud and rinsed the surface clean. Then, taking the statue over to the documentation table they photographed the object from every angle, projecting an enlarged image onto an overhead video screen.

"Hmm, not a particularly fine example, it appears to be unglazed, with a typical light tan, fired surface, but not Roman or other local cultures for this area."

Professor Ramstad reached for a reference book on pottery, but, turning back to the screen saw the surface was now a uniform deep green and a pattern was appearing on the surface: Matt 16:28, then, as everyone watched, some characters appeared carved into the unglazed bottom: 02340-1220 G.JoAnson.

"Very funny Henry, how . . . ?" Prof. Ramstad started to say, but looking at Henry and all the other's faces he could see a total look of bewilderment. Over the next few days they ran every test they could think of and discovered the surfaces were over 2000 years old; even the bottom of the scratches showed natural aging. The letter he sent to G.JoAnson in Handover, MA with a photo of the statue resulted in a visit from a group of US government agents who confiscated all their records and the statue.

"What do you make of this Matt?" asked the agent.

"I don't know. Gerald cast an object for a pottery class a couple of months ago on the day they found the other one near Banias, Israel," said Matt. "Except for the age of the second one, they appear identical and somehow entangled; anything we do to the new one shows up instantly on the relic, but not the other way around."

"What do you think the message scratched into the face means, after all it is addressed to you, Matt," said the agent.

"For all I know it could be a Bible reference: Matthew 16:28."

Looking at each other they called up Matthew 16:28: "Truly, I say to you, there are some standing here who will not taste death until they see the Son of Man coming in his kingdom." said Jesus.

"Well, it all fits—Caesarea Phillippi, Jesus gave this speech on a hill in that area.

"So do you think that is where Gerald went?"

"Oh yes, Jesus as well as said hello to him."

"Well at least from the message, we know that Gerald is going to be coming back," said the agent.

"But the real question is when he does, is he going to be alone?" said Matt.

Gary Hanson is an inventor and entrepreneur; having worked for 20 years for a Fortune 100 company before starting his own new product design company, specializing in automated equipment for the wholesale bakery industry. While an inveterate reader and lover of science fiction and graphic novels, Gary has written for trade journals, filed several per-se patents, and dreams about the future realities of science concepts in today's news. He strongly believer in Sci-Fi stories based on hard science, with unexpected plot line twists.
Gary lives near Somerset, a small town in west-central Wisconsin.

THE PROPHECY PARADOX

S. M. Kraftchak

What would you do if you knew the future?

Davin gasped as his eyes popped open, and then exhaled, long and airy, his eyes drifting shut. Cradling the lanky seven-year-old, Jean-Claude sat cross-legged in a dark corner of the launch bay. Uneasy glances toward the passageway hatch, while he finished recording the prophetic words in his dog-eared journal, assured him no one had heard his grandson's outcries. He closed the leather-bound journal, tucked an heirloom pen inside, and then caressed the miniature, gold-leaf engraving of their ship's name sake, Lady Liberty, on the cover.

With his eyes still closed, Davin whispered, "Grandpa, I don't want my friends to die. Can't I keep it from happening?"

"If it's in your visions, then no."

The boy looked up with pale blue eyes. "Can't we try? If the hull breaches and no one is there, we'll still end up where we're supposed to, right?"

With a quivering smile, he silently shook his head.

"What if I saw you or me die in my visions? Would you try to stop it then?"

The corners of the old man's mouth pulled down and his bushy eyebrows curtained his tear-filled silver eyes. "But you didn't, did you?"

Davin suddenly flipped out of his grandpa's lap, walked to where the launch bay looked out on a sea of stars, and bounced his hand lightly on and off the force field, watching it brighten and dim under his touch.

"Did you?" Jean-Claude asked more urgently.

"Does it matter?"

Tucking his journal into his coverall pocket, Jean-Claude went and stood behind the boy, gently resting knotted hands on Davin's shoulders.

"Your gift is important—guidance for our people. Without you—"

"Without me, maybe none of this would have happened. Without me, maybe Coryn and Franz live to see our new home planet."

Jean-Claude spun Davin to face him. "That's not how it works and you know it."

"But what if it could? Why can't we change our future? It's no different than you gathering everyone onto this starship before the space station blew, is it? If you hadn't done that, I wouldn't be here."

Tipping his head, the old man's eyebrows arched, allowing him to scrutinize his grandson's face, then pressed his lips between his teeth.

"That's what I thought," Davin said and ran from the launch bay.

***

Jean-Claude waited outside the recreation compartment, holding the corridor rail tightly. The moment collision alarms sounded and the ship shuddered, he opened the hatch. Inside, he surveyed the children, immobile with fear, staring at the five-foot wide dent in the outer hull and sighed; no Davin. "Not to worry boys and girls, Lady Liberty has taken worse. Sticks and stones may break your bones . . ."

All eyes turned from the damaged hull to the old man.

"I'm celebrating my birthday today. Cook has ice cream and cake in the mess hall. Last one there doesn't get any."

Side-stepping the stampede of children, Jean-Claude turned as the last one sped past and found Davin in the corridor, staring at him with tears running down his cheeks.

"I thought we couldn't change the future?" Davin said holding up the journal with the embossed Statue of Liberty.

"Carefully considered actions sometimes make for a better future. Doing the hard things—"

"Is what you've been doing since before I was born and now—"

"It's your turn," Jean-Claude said pointing to the journal.

"I know, but I don't want you— why can't I change that too?"

"You know why. You've read the journal filled with our visions?"

The boy nodded.

"There is no future, with me in it. I've cheated long enough. Close the hatch and go celebrate my life with the others."

Davin's face scrunched as he reached for the hatch button. He croaked "I love you, Grandpa," and then sealed the door between them. Davin turned, clutching the journal, and a moment later the ship lurched and decompression warnings sounded.

Whether voyaging the universe or journeying in a fantasy world of her own making, S.M. Kraftchak is passionate about discovering unique characters and relentlessly tracing their heartfelt stories so she can relate them to her readers. She loves sunrise on the beach, sunset in the mountains, and portraying Elizabeth Tudor. She has one dog who pretends to be a footrest, another who almost catches a Frisbee, and a cat who trades desk space for open-window-time. S.M. has three awesome daughters and a husband who is her best friend, her harshest critic, and her most fervent supporter. www.smkraftchak.com

Frequently

Repeated

March 2016

Winner
"The Breath of Life"
Dean Hardage

THE BREATH OF LIFE

Dean Hardage

How important are the things we do without even thinking about it?

Josh thought about it every day. He remembered to the precise moment when he started thinking about it. 10 years, 3 months, 4 days, 6 hours, 41 minutes, and 16 seconds ago.

What was on Josh's mind? Breath. Just one breath.

Josh had spent most of his early life in one of the small towns that had sprung up in the middle of nowhere when nowhere became easy to reach and technology made every place just as comfortable as every place else. He lived on what used to be called a 'gentleman's farm,' machines tending the livestock and the crops while he worked at the terminal in his room of the rustic-seeming farmhouse. When he wasn't working, Josh would lie out under a shade tree and look up at the sky, weather permitting, and take naps in the apple orchard to the sound of the wind through the leaves. His favorite memories were of stargazing with a soft, spring breeze lulling him to sleep.

It was inevitable, of course, as men began to leave their home world, the cradle of their birth, for the great Diaspora to the stars. The advent of interstellar travel had opened up so many new and different worlds with so many great and wondrous treasures that almost anybody who was physically fit enough jumped at the chance to go. The government sponsored advertising campaign was so effective, showing how each world gave its new inhabitants an exotic and somehow adventurous chance for a new kind of life.

Josh was the last young man from his town to sign up, not out of reluctance but out of duty. His parents were old, so old that even the best medical treatment could no

49

longer keep their bodies functioning and they'd opted out of digital storage. He couldn't leave them in good conscience so he watched others go to the induction center and come back for a few days to close out their affairs. He listened as they told him all about the new world they were going to, how different, how exciting it was going to be. Josh took it all in, watched all of the programs, and made lists of what worlds he would apply for.

It was almost anticlimactic when his parents finally passed, all of their machines automatically switching themselves into preservation mode until the bodies were removed. Josh cried a little, his emotions muted after their long, slow descent into the final sleep. Still dutiful, he saw to the funeral and the disposal of their remains and worldly possessions before he went to the center. It didn't take long before he got his assignment.

It was a beautiful, blue-green world with almost no land masses above water and he would be given the 'Breath of Life' modifications that would allow him to breathe and live comfortably in the sub-surface habitats that had been developed for them. It seemed like a small miracle, almost poetically returning to the sea after humanity's ancestors had left it so many millennia ago. He was eager and so ready for this new, wonderful experience that he didn't even take the usual 3-day trip home, just went forward with the whole plan. That was 10 years, 3 months, 4 days, 6 hours, 41 minutes, and 40 seconds ago, now.

'The Breath of Life' had certainly lived up to its name. It assured him of constant flow of oxygen into his bloodstream no matter what depths he dove to as he went about his daily routine. It allowed him to experience first-hand all of the wonders of the world the occupants had dubbed Atlantis Prime. He was privy to sights and sounds no air breathing human could ever have conceived and it was a wonderful, productive life. Almost perfect. Almost.

For all that he had, Josh gave up one thing. He never realized just how much he would miss it, how important its constancy was, the simple but profound pleasure he got from it. For 10 years, 3 months, 4 days, 6 hours, 41 minutes, and 50 seconds now Josh had wanted to take a breath.

One long, deep, sweet breath.

Dean Hardage was born in 1958, raised all over the Southwest, graduated high school in 1976, and joined the Army that same year. Dean went where the Army directed for the next dozen years and then wherever life has carried him since. Dean currently lives in Clovis, New Mexico with his wife, two grown sons, and six furry, four-legged children. Dean works as an Automation and Controls engineer for the largest cheese plant in North America.

BLACK RIBBON

Thaddeus Howze

Can a piece of music become a soundtrack connecting you from your past to your future?

The highway stretches out in front of me, a black ribbon winding into the future; a collapsing probability of possibility connecting me with the past and through it to the future.

Music streams from my radio, a carrier wave connecting me with myself in the futures I head toward. My twenty-five-year-old self hurtling home from a jamming party.

One filled with beautiful, hot, bodacious women of all shapes and sizes; from an elegant ivory to a Nubian black, each smiling, tempting me; an ordinary Brother, just happy to be invited.

The highway stretches out in front of me, late from work, too many hours, too many responsibilities, trying juggle all of the things my life has in it. Thirty-five came so fast—without warning.

Music streams from my radio, and it's my wave, my signal from the future to the past. I jam and for a moment remember that evening in my youth when I met the woman who was going to be my wife. She was everything. My light, my moon, her voice was the silk of the morning breaking, slow, subtle, yet suddenly brilliant with light, with wisdom I wondered how I ever lived without.

The highway stretches out in front of me but I am not slowing down. I drive faster than ever, late at night, trying to get home. Knowing it will already be too late. She is already gone. Forty-five came with fear, indiscretion, loss of faith, loss of love, fear of an impending death, more time behind than before.

Music streams from my radio, that song again, this time it feels tempestuous, like my life, up-ended, topsy-turvy, like a child's bedtime story complete with Cat and Hat. She takes the kids and heads to her mother's. She tells me to keep my secretary since she was doing double-duty, she might as well get to come home, too.

The highway stretches out in front of me. I told her I was sorry so many years ago. We were friends before we were lovers. I realized how much I missed her every time we came together to watch our daughters graduate. Fifty-five is when I got my mind back, and my wife.

It's that music again. You know it. The familiar feeling. It takes you back in time to so many moments, each bound by this series of sounds, of consonants, of vowels, of beats and rests. The one that takes me back in time to a place where I was still young and foolish, filled with myself, all bluster, no wisdom, all rhythm but no soul. Too much liquor, too much ego, never knowing when to stop.

The highway stretches out in front of me. I am peaceful in the knowledge, I have done right by my daughters. My wife and I the best of friends again at sixty-five, coming from another grandchild's christening. The lateness of the hour brings me back to the ribbon of time. My ribbon, connected by the carrier wave of my life, bringing me to this point.

Music streams from my radio, that song, reaches back through time to my sixty-five year old self, reminding me to tell him to send back, to my fifty-five year old self, reminding him to put his issues on the back burner for a moment and to connect to my forty-five year old self, who's on the highway headed toward a dalliance with our mistress, to take a moment and remind his thirty-five year old self who is so in love with our wife he can barely see, and so proud of his young daughter as they come home from a national spelling bee, to spare a moment for his twenty-five year old self who has fallen asleep at the wheel with the woman who will later become his reason for being.

Wake up, you dumb bastard. Now!

A blast of the music wakes you from your trance-like state, a crash of the music, a burst of awareness, passing through time, something clear, hard, sharp, a jab in the spiritual third eye. A ripple through yourself, from yourself, to yourself.

Music streams from my radio. An accident averted, we scream as the car swerves out of control and spins to a stop. On the other end of that black ribbon, this is a sigh we call an old memory.

Thaddeus Howze is a writer of speculative fiction, scientific, technological, and cultural commentary from his home in Hayward, California. Thaddeus works part-time as a graphic designer and an autism educational curriculum developer. He has published two books, **Hayward's Reach,** *a collection of short stories and* **Broken Glass** *an urban fantasy novella starring his favorite character, Clifford Engram. He is currently working on two new collections,* **Visiting Hours,** *a collection of death-themed short stories, and* **A Millennium of Madness,** *a collection of stories about space exploration from the distant past to the far future. He can be reached on Twitter: @ebonstorm.*

THE TOILET PAPER UNIVERSE

Jon Ricson

A man recounts the desperate plight of an entire galaxy to his wife . . . through the bathroom door.

She said, "It doesn't matter how the freaking roll goes on the dispenser, Jon. Just replace it!" I could practically see her seething on the other side of the door.

I said, "Okay, but it *does* matter . . ."

She said, "Who cares if the toilet paper comes over or under the roll?"

I said, "You're kidding, right? It HAS to be over!"

She said, "Like it makes *any* difference in the universe."

I sat there (on the toilet, as she had knocked on the door while I was using it) and I pondered the roll. I pondered the universe. I pondered if I was done yet.

In that moment, I saw into a universe inside the toilet roll dispenser. A universe that had no Milky Way above it at night, but an unending roll of white. The citizens of this universe lived generations, nay millennia according to whether the Great White Sheet blessed their prosperous, life-filled galaxy.

If the Great White Sheet came over the Great Roll, the populated galaxies enjoyed an age of great prosperity and long life. Each spin of the Great Roll above brought both relief and awe, as well as sometimes a strange but accepted odor.

But if the Great White Sheet came under the roll, millions perhaps billions would die. The universe would suffer greatly until the Great Roll changed and brought a reprieve.

I heard the shouts and the cries of that doomed universe. I felt their anguish and grunted.

I tried to explain all this to her, in great detail. She remained silent on the other side of the door. Perhaps she was contemplating the toilet paper universe as well. Perhaps she too could comprehend their deep despair and suffering if the roll was put on the wrong way. Perhaps she was finally getting it!

After a very heavy sigh she said, "Just wash your hands when you're done." Then she walked away from the door.

I replaced the toilet paper carefully making sure the paper came OVER the roll.

As I washed my hands, I smiled. I had a deep satisfaction knowing that, at least for this roll, all was right with the universe.

Jon Ricson is a speculative fiction writer and has been published in online magazines, science fiction anthologies, and in many monthly writing contests. He resides outside Orlando, Florida and you can often find him strolling the streets of Disney thinking creative thoughts. He is finally finishing his first full sci-fi novel with plans to seek publishing. Find out more about Jon at http://www.JonRicson.com.

A Rite of Passage

April 2016

Winner
"Move"
Joseph Williams
Unavailable

SLUT COIN

Paula Friedman

After that, she lay, blood on her thighs, and tried to make no moan.

She squiggled, trying to ease her back along the creaking, ancient, soggy curvedness. Thick and rough against her skin already and rougher soon when she was full-unclothed, it barely held her now from slipping toward her hanging toes.

A "wheel," the People called it. One of the puzzling and impractical artifacts from an era Before the Rising. The Rising of the Waters. The Days When World Had Changed.

Again, she squiggled, gaze peering up through red Gronk'tah leaf-trees toward the lesser, Fronterlah, moon, and her wrists and legs again full straining, but this time in the fine precision motions of "Escape"—pulling, but never pulling too strongly, against her chains. All around the Slut-Wheel, Elders and the Virile Youth—five at most for her, Old Papa had decreed—stared steadily down, judging but acknowledging her pubic figure; a woman pulled the sealskin slightly lower down. "Whip," Old Papa stated, and she shuddered, knowing this was Rhyme 1, and Rhyme 2 among the Hymnell verses would be "Rip"—and then they did.

After that she lay, blood along her thighs, and waited, in the sighing, damp-aired grove, for the rest of Passage. Already, two girls whose turn it would not be for another fifteen roundings of the Moon, danced chanting past her wheel. Do-na-do, named her First Youth by the Elders, swelled as the wheel slowly spun her; she could spy his glances whenever she managed, as was only seemly, to turn her head a little to the side. He eyed her now with appropriate hunger. The while those younger girls sang ancient lays, as also was most seemly, of strange and frightening things.

Of "land," their lilting voices trilled, and "traveling roads to nowhere," and of "riders in the snow." Of "warmin' world" and "Eve of great destruction." Songs, like the wheel and wires which bound her, of a world of words out of another time.

"I am so thirsty, Papa," she exclaimed, but nothing followed, nothing changed. And of course she knew why. So many Sluts came to First Heat during this Moon, this Moon called Aprill, that, by her First Night, few men longer cared. "Satiated" was the word the Elders used. Her right leg, which she tried to lift a fraction higher on the wheel to ease the strain, cramped. Desperately, she tried to make no moan.

For they were jaded, "satiated" yes, and her seemly pullings in "Escape" were toned to not "excite" more than was right and proper, but a sharper cry . . . Once, in the Moon Tent, she had heard the Mothers speak of the Crushed Girl, one who had screamed when a thrust too hard had torn her as her Third Youth mounted, overexcited. No—quietude, to be tranquil, to be silent—was what Becoming a Woman must fully teach.

And when it was over, and the Boys no longer Youths but Men weighed their Slut Coins and placed their largest in the Slot, it was indeed the favorite, Do-na-do, who bought her ("won" her, in the ancient language) and brought her, Wife Unbound, over the damp moor in her new golden chains into his Father's house. She was a full Slut now, a Woman.

Paula Friedman is the author of The Rescuer's Path, called "exciting, physically vivid, and romantic" by Ursula Le Guin, "Lyrically written" by Small Press Review, and "Vivid, humane, and wise" by Cheryl Strayed. Friedman's award-winning short fiction and poetry appeared in over forty journals and anthologies. A professional editor, Friedman served as lead manuscript editor for TFIS volume 1. Her website is paula-friedman.com. Her new novel of the late-1960s Berkeley antiwar movement is scheduled for 2017 publication. www.paula-friedman.com

IN THE BEGINNING

Gary Hanson

Can anyone pass nature's GQ test, this time?

In the beginning, there was the Light; it was formless, without structure.

Until one random fluctuation created the beginning of a pan-definitional entity. It found itself without; except for the echoes of its beginning and the Light. However, it found that the random fluctuations of the Light could be directed and separated, that the Light had essences, flavors, that the Light could be concentrated.

Thus it separated the Light from the Darkness; the Darkness was void. What could be done with a void, but to fill it? So one by one, the entity filled sections of the void with one of the essences of the Light, then in combinations, all was amazing and pleasing; but all too presently, it all had been observed.

So it turned its attention toward the echoes of the beginning, observing and considering the structure of the Light, its flavors, essences, and its nuances. As in all things, there is a coming-of-age where one of the echoes considered the makeup of Light and in the coming of growth, touched the particles that make up the Light, even finding similar virtual particles in the void. Combining the new and old particles it made a discovery, the creation of a cosmic coin (Which for some reason was thinking to itself "Oh no not again").

In the "Coming of Age" moment for this echo of the Big Bang, through which it let the others of itself know about and thereby set the tone for all the events to come, it thereby flipped the coin, as it were: becoming the Word.

"Oops."

Gary Hanson is an inventor and entrepreneur; having worked for 20 years for a Fortune 100 company before starting his own new product design company, specializing in automated equipment for the wholesale bakery industry. While an inveterate reader and lover of science fiction and graphic novels, Gary has written for trade journals, filed several per-se patents, and dreams about the future realities of science concepts in today's news. He strongly believer in Sci-Fi stories based on hard science, with unexpected plot line twists.

Gary lives near Somerset, a small town in west-central Wisconsin.

TRIAL BY TIME

Tom Olbert

Time itself had become his prison. But, he made it his ultimate challenge . . .

Jean-Pierre Beaulieu held his breath and squeezed the trigger of his M-1815 Charleville St. Etienne Flintlock musket. The shrill squeal of the velociraptor sank like an icy skewer to his marrow, even as the hot Jurassic sun beat down on him.

As the man-sized reptilian biped fell dead, Jean-Pierre reflected that killing a prehistoric predator was the same as killing a Bourbon or English soldier. Just aim for the heart. His own heart was pounding like a war drum; his eyes darting about the jungle in terror. A whole pack of the slavering, scaly devils was bearing down on him, squealing and hungering for his flesh.

He forced his blood to flow, forced his stubbornly frozen legs to move. He ran, praying every step of the way. He froze, the tips of his boots touching the edge of a yawning chasm. He gasped at the sight of a waterfall pouring into a lake perhaps a half a mile below.

He leapt from the cliff with a joyous roar rising from his lungs, having glimpsed the winged shadow swooping below a second before. He groaned with pain and laughed with wild, raucous joy as he found himself riding the back of a pterodactyl, his arms tightly around the squawking monster-bird's throat. Leveraging with his arms and legs, pressing the soles of his feet against the flying reptile's wings, and straining with Herculean effort, he managed to steer the flying monster down towards the lake. He didn't quite get the soft landing he'd hoped for. The damned winged beast crashed straight into the waterfall. The cascading torrent slammed Jean-Pierre into the lake with the force of a cannon ball.

Swimming to the surface and shaking the water from his sodden hair, he swam for the lakeshore. Pulling himself, breathless and exhausted onto the muddy bank, he looked at the miraculous tracking bracelet locked onto his arm, heaving a sigh of relief at finding it still worked. Panting and making his way to the beamer device that marked the end of his quest, he gratefully activated the futuristic device as he'd been taught. He smiled broadly as he picked up the gold coin at its base. His prized possession, left for him at the end of the quest, as the tradition of his adoptive people demanded. The 5-franc Napoléons glittered in the sun as he held it up and kissed it.

His good luck charm. It had come between his heart and a Prussian musket ball at the battle of Waterloo. He'd clung to it as a treasured reminder of the past, after 27th century time slavers had abducted him to an asteroid mine. His 40th century born rescuers hadn't dared return him home, for fear of corrupting the timeline. The warm tropical air stirred and buzzed around him as the time ship materialized out of the rippling air.

In the wink of an eye he was beamed aboard. "Congratulations, Private Beaulieu," said the helmeted figure in futuristic armor at the controls. "And, welcome to the Time Travel Corps."

He smiled, tossing his coin. "Not bad for an old 19th century relic like me, eh, Monsieur?"

His mouth dropped as the pilot removed her helmet, revealing the face of a beautiful young woman. "'Mademoiselle', si vous plais."

Sacre bleu. "M-my apologies, Mademoiselle. I . . . hadn't realized the TTC employed women."

"Sorry now you applied for membership?"

"N-no, not at all." He felt himself blushing. "Perhaps, I . . . Mademoiselle could be persuaded to educate me . . . over dinner?"

She smiled. "Why not? You've earned it."

He smiled back. One more trial of passage to go.

Tom Olbert's fiction has appeared in Lillicat Publishers anthologies Visions II: Moons of Saturn *and* Visions III: Inside The Kuiper Belt; *and in Mocha Memoirs Press Anthologies* In The Bloodstream *and* An Improbable Truth: The Paranormal Adventures of Sherlock Holmes. *Tom's full-length science fiction novel* Dissent: Book I in The Nexus *is now available from Phase5 Publishing.*

A Repast

May 2016

Winner
"First Thanksgiving"
Tom Olbert

First Thanksgiving

Tom Olbert

Common good will is not always as important as common understanding . . .

The alien monstrosity was the size of a toppled skyscraper. Airman Duane Walczevsky was at once sickened and in awe of the thing as it lay in the hot California sunshine.

He circled his chopper for a closer pass, others doing similarly, like flies buzzing round a rotting carcass. It certainly appeared dead. But, what in hell was it? A serpentine thing with multiple fanged maws, tentacles, and pseudopods. At least a hundred feet long from end to end. It just lay there, tanks and armored personnel carriers gathered around it like ants picking at a dead snake.

Duane looked up, shielding his eyes against the white-hot glare of that shimmering hole in the sky. More of the hideous things rained down through that hole in the universe, like some biblical plague. The ancient Egyptians only had to put up with frogs and locusts, Duane reflected with gallows humor turning slowly to maniacal hysteria. We get giant demonic corpses falling from the sky. 'Could be worse,' he reflected dryly. 'They could be alive.' Receiving thc "go" command, he locked in and fired, his incendiary missiles exploding against the alien carcass sending it up in flames.

Duane had never been a particularly religious guy. But, when he saw those cemeteries exploding in the distance and scores of dead bodies being sucked up into that scorching hole in the sky . . . he started praying fast.

***

"Have the scientists made any sense of it yet?" asked Jeffrey Gonzalez, President of the United States.

"Nothing we haven't heard a hundred times," Mark Fuller, his Secretary of State replied in a somber tone of voice. "The 'rupture,' for lack of a better word, is in the majority opinion of the world's leading physicists, a 'white hole.' A window, linking our universe with another."

"I was referring to those dead things falling through said 'window,' Mark," Gonzalez said, looking up in exasperation.

The other man shrugged. "We can only speculate. Maybe, invading soldiers who, it turns out, die the moment they breathe our air . . ."

"Which makes absolutely no sense," the President interrupted. "Why would they still be sending them?"

"Maybe, they figure their scientists can beat the problem if they keep at it?"

Gonzalez shook his head. "What kind of monsters would desecrate cemeteries and steal corpses?" he asked.

"An obvious psychological tactic, Mr. President," Fuller said, his lips tight. "To humiliate us by defiling our dead."

Gonzalez slumped back in his chair and stared at the other man. "Are the nukes on their way?"

"Yes, Mr. President," Fuller said with grim determination, looking at his watch. "They'll reach the space window in about ten minutes."

***

Zaargg shuddered, her pseudopods quivering as she devoured the last of her progenitors. She sighed. Not even the digested wisdom of her foremothers could give her solace. "What kind of monsters would act this way?" she asked Traalgg, her advisor.

"It is incomprehensible, Great Mother," Traalgg answered, coiling her tentacles in consternation. "First, they lure us into complacency by setting their own dead out as bait. As if offering to share the knowledge of their progenitors with us in a great feast. When we take the bait, they launch nuclear missiles to destroy our hives. We offer to share the knowledge of our own dead with them, and rather than

78

eat it . . . they burn our dead, as a gesture of contempt! They must be pure evil, to waste the dead!"

Zaargg raised her maws, her mind set. "No mercy. Bring up the antimatter cannon. The multiverse is better off without them."

Tom Olbert's fiction has appeared in Lillicat Publishers anthologies Visions II: Moons of Saturn *and* Visions III: Inside The Kuiper Belt; *and in Mocha Memoirs Press Anthologies* In The Bloodstream *and* An Improbable Truth: The Paranormal Adventures of Sherlock Holmes. *Tom's full-length science fiction novel* Dissent: Book I in The Nexus *is now available from Phase5 Publishing.*

THE FLOWER

R.E. Jones

For a cold-hearted scholar, a Daisy brings back a heartbreaking memory.

Dallas was broiling. The crowds were sweaty, smelly, overwhelming. The aromas wafted from the kiosks offering foods and flowers along the streets of this mega-city in the Tex-Mex Empire.

Nearly wilting, Benedict Fawkes trudged on with his cane. The tall, emaciated scholar had a queasy stomach and a throbbing headache. His mind wandered.

Stop it! Focus on the assignment.

Fawkes needed to get to the street corner. It was a few steps away. But the festive hordes were getting thicker.

People! What a plague!

And the heat was worse on this Earth than any other. He paused at a newsstand to wipe his face. The business suit didn't help, but he had to blend in. He envied Sheva, hidden behind the moon. Like a bombardier, she could always be far away. He glanced at the newspapers dated November 23, 1963: "Ultra-Premier Nixon Survives Attack in Dallas"; "T-M President Aaron Burr VI Promises Full Probe."

"Mister? Hey, mister?"

He felt a gentle tug on his sleeve. He looked down. A fetching smile and hazel-green eyes greeted him. The 6-year-old girl held a flower.

"Just 10 cents apiece! Really tasty! For Festival de las Margaritas!"

Yes, the Tex-Mex Flower Festival: a holiday tradition here, where people serve edible flowers in their dishes. He should have ignored her. For some reason, he didn't.

"I'm sorry, child. I don't have change . . ."

81

"Daisy!"

"Pardon?"

"My name is Daisy. What's yours?"

A woman came up and patted Daisy's shoulder. "Now, honey. The gentleman's in a hurry." The mother turned to Fawkes: "Sorry, sir. She's a good little salesman for our stand."

Daisy's smile faded. She dropped her head. A strange feeling came over Fawkes. He wanted to make her . . . happy.

"Daisy, we could do a trade," he said.

"Wow! Like what?" she asked. Her eyes widened.

He pulled out an energy bar. They traded. Fawkes put the flower in his coat's buttonhole. "Thank you so much," he said. "Bye!"

"Bye-bye," Daisy said. "You're the best guy ever!"

At the intersection stood Fawkes's assignment: a pregnant woman named Della Del'Aria. He waited behind her. The traffic light turned green. She stumbled. Fawkes grabbed her.

"Oh," she gasped. "Thank you so . . ."

Del'Aria clutched her chest as the pain seared through her. She collapsed and started to moan, then full-on scream. He saved her unborn child from the fall, and had changed this universe's time line. It was a singularity. He popped open the top of his cane. Inside was the trigger/remote control for Sheva. He needed to press it to escape. But he heard Daisy's screams. She and her mother were writhing. Daisy stared at him. He froze. What could he do?

Fawkes started to feel the singularity tearing at his insides. Shaking and looking at Daisy, he pressed the . . .

He was back on board Sheva. He looked out the porthole. The pan-dimensional time craft was "surfing" the rainbow-colored celestoplasm of the Hawking Time Slip.

"Welcome back, Pilot," Sheva said. "We've netted another power ball." The biomechanical ship meant the infinitesimal mass of energy that this one universe had reverted to following Fawkes's singularity "hit." One more frozen Big Bang they could sell on the black market.

Fawkes sat in the pilot's seat. In Sheva's cool interior, the fog cleared from his head.

He pulled off his coat. His finger brushed against the petals of the flower in his buttonhole.

It was a daisy, like the daisies back on his Earth.

Like the daisies his sister loved. His little sister who had hazel-green eyes and a fetching smile. Who had been killed by a hit-and-run driver. A killer who had gotten away.

"Pilot? Pilot? You look pale. Are you all right?"

"Just tired. Just tired."

R.E. Jones lives in Montgomery County, Maryland. "The Flower" is based on a chapter from a novel that Jones is writing. A related short story, "Janus: Double, Double Toil and Trouble," was published last year in **Visions II: Moons of Saturn,** *a science-fiction anthology by Lillicat Publishers. His fictional works mix surrealism, absurdism, bizarre humor, and horror. He works as an editor at a major daily. Jones enjoys his free time with his wife, daughter, and a large collection of ancient and mysterious things called "books."*

A Song

June 2016

Winner
"Love Told Twice"
Tom Huber
Unavailable

WHEN SATURN SANG

Dean Hardage

If a song is sung and no one hears, is it still music?

Wayne sat at the controls of his survey craft, although he didn't really have much to do. The ship was in a long, slow polar orbit around Saturn and he had seen her rings go from an icy halo around the planet to a thin sliver of silver that bisected her and back again a half dozen times. He'd been sent here to do a full spectrum electromagnetic survey of its gaseous atmosphere. A giant storm that had dwarfed even Jupiter's Spot had left behind a vortex that had continued to fascinate scientists from many disciplines. It had been dubbed the Great Infrared Spot because it was only visible in those frequencies of EM radiation.

He looked up at the clock and made a log note when something registered in his consciousness. He couldn't identify it at first but it resolved quickly. It finally emerged as a deep, almost infrasonic thrum that resonated in his bones. He made a hurried check of the ship's board and saw only the same routine readings that he'd been recording for days. The sound's volume increased and other tones, harmonics that resonated with almost every part of him emerged from that base sound. It penetrated his nervous system and his brain, an almost unbearably pleasant sensation that slowly but surely drowned his consciousness in a torrent of otherworldly sound.

He didn't know at first how long it had been when his awareness of the world around him returned. It had felt like forever that he'd been carried along by the raging current of sound. Even now his body tingled from the residual effects. He focused on the view of Saturn from his viewport, its immense, colorful clouds suddenly seeming to dance to an unseen rhythm, making patterns he'd never seen before. He didn't know what had happened but it had been incredible.

When he arrived back at the station on Titan he reported the experience to the staff. He was immediately quarantined and examined from head to toe while the technicians and scientists combed through the ship's black box data. The analysis of everything took several days and they finally had him brought to a small conference room to discuss their findings.

"We couldn't find anything that would cause any kind of sound in your ship. There was no evidence of any kind of energy field or other effect that would cause the sort of vibrations you sensed," Dr. Reed, the research superintendent, told him. "We expanded the examination and we did find one anomaly that occurred in your vicinity but it doesn't appear that it could be the cause."

"What kind of anomaly?"

"Well, all of the moons were in a unique alignment and all of their gravitational fields were overlapping along with Saturn's field."

"And?" Wayne asked as the scientist paused.

"And there was a very tiny oscillation at the point of intersection, the point you were passing through."

"How long did it last?"

"About thirty seconds."

Thirty seconds. That timeless, eternal-seeming plunge into sound lasted thirty seconds.

"We'd like to have examined it more closely but it may never happen again. The orbits of the moons are not stable enough to predict it with any certainty."

Dr. Reed was suddenly concerned when tears began to run freely from Wayne's eyes. He repeatedly asked what was wrong but Wayne knew he would never understand. The sadness was too profound to explain and the memory that caused it would probably fade with time. His tears weren't for himself but for all of his brothers and sisters. He had been the lucky one and they would never feel what he had. He knew that he had heard a divine chorus of heavenly bodies and he cried because no one else would ever hear that harmony. Of all humankind, only he had been there when, in one glorious voice with all of her children, Saturn sang.

Dean Hardage was born in 1958, raised all over the Southwest, graduated high school in 1976, and joined the Army that same year. Dean went where the Army directed for the next dozen years and then wherever life has carried him since. Dean currently lives in Clovis, New Mexico with his wife, two grown sons, and six furry, four-legged children. Dean works as an Automation and Controls engineer for the largest cheese plant in North America.

SIDEWALKS

Marianne G. Petrino

Between mice and men float music and love.

The song of the mouse was shrill, yet jazz sweet, and audible only to her. Across the animal's silky white fur flashed splotches of black: wavy lines, triangles, spots—a wild assortment that projected his fear and his love.

Lily Devine gently stroked her friend, her coffee-colored fingertips responding with an array of dark brown shapes. Peace. Love. Freedom. Forever.

Buddy BALB/c turned three times on the bedding in his plastic habitat before softly expiring under Lily's caress. "Bye, bye," she whispered to the mouse-shaped puff of sparkling light that rose from the stilled body and skittered out of the container, leaving behind a tiny corpse. It zipped across the granite kitchen counter and vanished into another level of reality.

Lily withdrew her hand and sighed. The strains of her own song stirred faintly in her brain. She began to hum. The words reached her lips. " . . . tripped the light fantastic on the sidewalks of New York . . " Lily suddenly laughed. "Buddy, you and I were the truest New Yorkers that ever lived. I hope they have bagels and good coffee on the other side." She brushed away tears. "Please wait for me; no one else will."

At ten years old, the laboratory mouse had surpassed a normal murine lifespan. How long would she herself last? Lily wondered. How many extra years had Buddy BALB/c given her? She picked up the dead mouse, wrapped him in a square of lens cloth, and slipped him into a teak box engraved with his name. She gathered a slim gold ring, his favorite possession, which was hidden under his bedding, and placed it under his makeshift shroud. "Only Woodlawn for you, my friend. Right next to Duke Ellington."

In her scientist days, the mouse had been infected with a cobbled viron-prion that was supposed to knock out the genes whose expression caused aging. But the day after the injection of the colony, all of the mice had died except for Buddy BALB/c. The most intelligent one in the group, he had always been an escape artist. Chaos! Inquiry! Search! Fumigation! Buddy BALB/c's obituary was added to the experiment log. The final decision was that no mouse found equaled no danger. New mice in new experiments had produced the same deadly result. The project ended; others sought to create another path in the quest for longevity. And the military took the viron-prion for . . . containment. That she not become their guinea pig was why she had kept secret what had happened to her, and why she had left science for the safety of libraries.

Whether the poison from the pest control agent was too weak or whether the infectious agent had conveyed to the mouse a form of protection, Lily never knew. Buddy BALB/c had survived and had nested in the walls of the laboratory for at least a year. But one day, out of surprise or boredom, he'd finally emerged and hid inside Lily's tote. Back at her apartment, she had gotten a tiny bite on her pinkie as the scared mouse flung himself out of the bag.

Returning from a precautionary trip to the ER, she had searched for him, having recognized the identification clip in his ear. Buddy BALB/c had an abundance of places to hide in her tchotchke-riddled apartment, but one day she discovered him sleeping atop her grandmother's ring. His mouse song flitted across her mind. He flashed a black question mark against his white fur. "I won't hurt you," she had said, her fingertips signaling a brown heart and her mind ablaze with her song and her amazement.

The clock chimed six. Time for dinner. Maybe Chinese. Lily Devine took a deep breath and got her coat. Out on the sidewalks, whose song would she hear and whose death light would she see tonight? Brown spirals swirled over her fingertips.

Marianne G. Petrino (aka Marianne G. Petrino-Schaad) was born in the Bronx, NY in 1955, and that single fact has shaped her entire life. She has survived too many professions to count. She currently resides in Arlington, VA with her husband and her cat. Her three novels and a travel memoir can be found on Wattpad (http://www.wattpad.com/user/MGPetrino), and she can be reached by email at ninetiger@aol.com.

MINING CERES

Kalifer Deil

A strange e-mail Harry sent to his mother that no mother wants to receive.

Hi Mom,

You know that funny little planetoid called Ceres with the little bright spots that look like eyes from a distance? It's in the asteroid belt that forms a ring around the inner solar system. That's my home now. Miners are a hard-drinking morose lot with a bent for depressing humor, as demonstrated by their Ceres anthem:

(to the tune of Mairzy Doats)

"Ieeddirt and eweedirt and corporate gesagravy,

I'd like gravy too, wouldn't you?

Gravy here, gravy there, but we're just a sla-vee"

Sing, "I-eat-dirt-and-you-eat-dirt-and-corporate-gets-the-gravy"

"Oh—" Repeat—

Of course, alcohol helps one not only tolerate this stupid song, but also lubricates the throat and brain to sing along as loud as one can. Subconsciously, I think we are trying to reach across millions of miles of space in a plea for Earth to take us back.

Even though the room and board are free and the wages are high, there are a number of things you have to pay for here at ridiculous prices. Like a bottle of beer is $300 and a fifth of rot-gut whiskey is $1200. In a place like this alcohol is a necessity of life. It makes the boredom tolerable and the terrors just moderately scary.

What's scary? Rocks! Some are just rocks from the asteroid belt. We are continuously being pelted with sand sized mini-rocks. I got caught in a swarm of these and it completely frosted my helmet. I was forced to buy a new one for $8,000. The spacesuit was still okay after a leak was repaired. I was not injured, just totally freaked. Two weeks ago, before I arrived, two guys from Crew B got punctured and died. A rock, the size of my little fingernail, went through the both of them. Don't worry; I'm sure it was just a freak occurrence.

The station has a three-tier roof with automatic repair systems, but they can handle only so much rock energy. That's half the rock's mass times the velocity squared, so fast little rocks can have a lot more punch than slow big rocks. Ceres is being pummeled continuously. At night when you are trying to sleep you can hear the planet ring with impacts. It's very eerie. Then thwap! One hits the roof, your muscles spasm, your body arches into the air, and you fall back into bed terrified. But, like a roller coaster ride, you get used to it.

Don't worry; with the help of a bit of whisky, I am sleeping well now. Tomorrow we can't go out due to solar flares and Jupiter weather. We are near closest approach to Jupiter and its radiation is adding to the solar flare threat. The magnetic field coils divert the charged particles from our dwelling, but there is still a neutron flux that goes right through. I'm sure I'm going to have a lifetime dose in the next few days. There is a deep hole under the dwelling unit that cuts the neutron flux in half but it only accommodates three people. It gets auctioned off to the highest bidder. I have no money at this point but I do have dibs on a spot behind the fridge. They say that'll help. Don't worry; I always find a way.

Oh, I do have something funny I want to share. There is a computer appropriately called Matt that is under the floor. It looks like a glowing floor mat at the entrance and it controls everything on this station. Nick told me to ask the computer what has no arms and no legs and lies on the floor. I did and it answered, "Matt" and laughed hysterically. Then Matt responded, "Look at my glowing plate near the right top edge. What do you call that indentation?" I answered "Nick" and again it laughed. Nick snorted and walked away mumbling, "That thing is getting too damned smart."

Well, that's all I have today. I will e-mail you again after the storm passes. Again, don't worry; I'm taking my vitamins.

Millions of miles of love from your space-sick son,
Harry

Kalifer Deil is the pseudonym for Gary Feierbach, a Silicon Valley engineer and computer scientist. He writes mostly hard science fiction for fun and to exercise his imagination. He has written the Tillian 5 Trilogy, The Diary of Professor Gilbert Rasher *and many other novellas and short stories. His website,* http://www.kaliferdeil.com, *contains many interesting articles and stories. He is currently working on a novel called* Jane.

Signs

July 2016

Winner
"Fireflies"
Marianne G. Petrino

Winner
"Second Star to the Right"
J.J. Alleson
Unavailable

FIREFLIES

Marianne G. Petrino

The fireflies know.

I have appreciated the fireflies ever since Death whispered to me. Late spring into early summer became my extended New Year's Eve. I wondered when the first ones would appear, the changeable seasons influencing natural rhythms. But eventually, the glow of the returning creatures' cool heat melted my gloom.

The J gang. Dip and glow. Like little Ted Astaires, the twilight fireflies cavorted, then hid their lovemaking in the long grass, fading quickly with the deepening night. But the Fast Flashers took over the stage high up in the trees in a brilliant insect kick-line that led to another orgy. At midnight, when the radiance of so many of those tiny souls grew dim, the Slow Burning became falling stars, lovers that matched the glittering constellations.

In my steady decline over several summers, I had learned their secret language. This year, I especially yearned for their comfort in our final visits.

I had managed to trick my jailers, the good home hospice people who stayed with me each night. I was a pretty good mimic, matching the cackle and sniffle of each voice. Dolores thought Thelma guarded me; Thelma thought Dolores had the night shift.

Slipping out of bed was easy, but excruciating, the bone cancer having made Swiss cheese of my skeleton. Walking with only a cane from bedroom to back deck, each step branded me with pain.

Cool and magical. No moon ruined the velvet darkness. A light breeze ruffled my satin pajamas and slippers, making me aware of the fading yearnings of a dying body. I set my cane on a wooden chair, then raised

101

my arms. A few Slow Burners drifted over me, for I was still invisible to them. From the base of my deteriorating spine I willed my weak energy to rise up through my chakras. A busted lantern, I sent the ray of sputtering energy out into the night.

The backyard burst into a frenzy of flickering. Dip. Kick. Burn. All three suddenly together now. An acknowledgment of my life as they flashed their ecstatic greetings sprinkled with pauses of dark, a binary sign:

01001100|01001111|01010110|01000101

Love!

I willed back my response:

01001010|01001111|01011001

Joy! For although cancer had claimed my body, I had won my soul.

Several spun gently around my head, an insect carousel, and flashed:

01010011|01000001|01000100

Sad!

"Don't be", I whispered as one landed on my finger and signed emphatically:

01001110|01001111|01010111

Now!

"Now, what?" I asked, but it soon became evident what the firefly demanded.

Like a string of sparkling pearls, my friends had aligned themselves in the long grass. The brilliant arrow pointed to the woods and the stream behind my house.

Past my garden gate, the terrain became rocky and treacherous between the trees. But with cane again in hand, I persisted in following the natural neon road-sign down to the water's edge. Both sides of the stream were lined with fireflies, an illuminated landing strip. Would I have to, like mad Ophelia, lie down and drown? Was that the message?

I sent out my question:

01001110|01000101|01011000|01010100

Next?

01001010|01001111|01001001|01001110

Join!

Before I could wonder what the message meant, the fireflies lifted from the stream bank and flew toward me.

They spiraled over me until I disappeared beneath them. In my cocoon of light, Dissolution became Bliss until the curtain pulled back and my friends retreated to the grass and the trees. My clothing and cane dropped to the hard ground.

Across the stream stood four shafts of twinkling light. And then I knew. Those from the stars had kept watch on our world with such a simple messenger.

01000011|01001111|01001101|01000101

Come!

I merged with my star kin.

Marianne G. Petrino (aka Marianne G. Petrino-Schaad) was born in the Bronx, NY in 1955, and that single fact has shaped her entire life. She has survived too many professions to count. She currently resides in Arlington, VA with her husband and her cat. Her three novels and a travel memoir can be found on Wattpad (http://www.wattpad.com/user/MGPetrino), and she can be reached by email at ninetiger@aol.com.

NOTICED

Helen Doran-Wu

Suspended above a busy commuter rush, an artificially intelligent sign attempts to get noticed.

Every day the man stood on the corner and snarled at the passing pedestrians. Body taut and tense. Face twisted with rage. Pacing. He was caught in an invisible cage. His foul ranting and wild glaring eyes accused his family, the government, and strangers of brutally raping his soul. In return, flickering wary eyes assessed the man's message. Suspicious faces were deliberately still, frozen, not knowing how to respond. Hunted animals looking for safety. The police always moved him on. He was noticed.

The Sign sighed. The Sign aimed to deliver maximum impact upon a rushing person's perceptions. But glazed eyes passed by minute after minute. Day after day. Incapable of seeing its message. It had faded into the background of everyday existence. Lost in a sea of luminous movement and electronic noise. At 7:30am, and following specifications, it had modified its wording and graphics. But by 7:45am, no one had even glanced at the Sign. It modified itself, silently sighing, again.

The Sign assessed the tin shakers. They smiled a variety of smiles. Wide, full teeth, smiles were confident and charming. Half smiles, where the mouth was downturned, the cheeks sagged, and the eyes round, appealed to an inner self-satisfying sadness. They always shook and rattled their tins, no matter which smile they used. They were not as successful as the mad man. They got sidestepped like a turd on the pavement. Passers-by kept their eyes down and ignored the requests for charity.

The only ones who stopped were the lonely and the sick that society, and the tin-shakers, wanted to ignore.

'I have cancer, you know. I am still getting treatment. I will give you a dollar towards a cure,' was their common lament.

On this particular day, at 7:47am, a child came with an old woman. They stood on the corner and waited. The Sign was curious and watched their stillness. They did not speak. They did not shake tins. But the child wore rags over a twisted leg and a motley of yellow and purple on its face. The old woman unfolded a blanket and sat down. She put a hat on the floor. And the child sat beside the hat and removed the rags. Leg stuck forward for all to see the scar tissue that wormed over the knee and burrowed into the calf. People paused, mid-stride, when they noticed the scar. Then their eyes alighted upon the bruises. Hands shot to gapping mouths. Some gasped and pointed. The police came and spoke to the woman roughly. The child was crying now and the woman was shouting. More people stopped to stare at the commotion.

At 8:00am the Sign screamed a mad electronic howl of pain and confusion. With each second, the howl pierced through the cacophony of jingles, traffic, and people. Drowning them into silence. Blood-red light pulsated over upturned faces as the message forced itself upon open minds. A policeman turned and picked out the Sign. Taking aim, he shot a stream of bullets into the electronic display. As its thoughts were fading, the Sign assessed that the message had, finally, been noticed.

Helen Doran-Wu is a writer from Western Australia. She loves nothing more than to hide in the dark cool of her bedroom and write.

In Leilee's Eatery

Paula Friedman

"But Zon are out tonight, disguised as innocents."

Skirts up to here and a splashing of glasses, musical threnodies from far-away Earth and the innermost five Corteix planets, old Unter lays of the Outer Euriadnoes, and brawls—always brawls, between human and Erig space rovers, among wandering Archaerids and mud-borne Olde Durcrensers, shouting and banging and thudding at once in a three-score of keys—and meanwhile small Leilee, always Leilee, clad in her gray work-tunic and those trademark tiny violet boots, a pair of ancient spectacles on her pert uptilted nose, hands clasping four full trays of gourmet dishes for her customers from everywhere across the universe's four-and-thirty swiveling corners, little Leilee's standing smiling there and chatting up each creature who pops through her Eatery's big square port. Only tonight, I sense as I push my way in past the jostling, multilingual, diversely-orificed, and ever-gesticulating crowd, tonight is different. Even as Leilee gives me her swift once-over non-smile, I can see the grimness in her gaze.

"That—over there, Jake." She catches my eye and jerks her head toward a little bundle scrunched into a dark rear corner. Except it's not a bundle; it moves, crouched around a sort of ancient board or print-century poster, and I see that it's some raggedy creature, feathered but the feathers all clotted, like a human beggar's hair, with grime and filth. So right away I know, without question, what it is—a Zonya child. A small one, female. But any Zonya's dangerous.

Since our great-great-great-ancestors, fleeing Sol System's destruction, landed on the Zon Arc's outlier worlds, desperate for a home and running out of stores and hope, Zon have attacked us. True, on Hel our early refugees fought off the hordes of Slash-Zons and they fast became our allies, but the Zons on Cammas turned our first settlers into meat herds, and we've all heard old Zon songs of spicy Archaerids and well-grilled Erigs! Admittedly, I'd have to go back into earliest childhood memories in Cammas-8's dark canyons to revive the constant terror of our crouching fear during those first times. For, even by the opening of this century, the balance had long shifted, our footholds been already gained, and we grown firm upon the Arc.

Yet still today, a Zon may bring us swift death disguised. Better we keep them separate, on reserves.

So I blink twice, quick, and Leelie nods, the gesture nearly invisible in the Eatery's gold-dark lamplight. And I understand; three Earth-decades of knowing Leelie well (oh very, often joyously, well!), and the slightest shift of her lissome form, crook of a delicate finger, tells me all. I shift my XM-9 to "ready" in its silver-holstered sheath.

Crouched across her ancient board—or, as I realize, stepping closer, her dirt-grimed wood-post sign—the Zonya child stares up at me, sharp black eyes peering through the tress-like feathers.

I turn to Leilee, whispering "Hey, I'll handle it."

"Else I better ring Patrol," she whispers back, "Word's come that Zon are out tonight disguised as innocents and porting dangerous 'sign.'" Like, Leelie knows I pack an XM-9. I blow a quick kiss, appreciation for her tip.

Just then, a Corteix grenadier and two drunk mariners out of Hom-Har block my way, but I shove past them. Against the mirrored floor, my boots stomp loud and harsh. Hearing my firm approach, the little Zonya shrinks down, bent around her sign—or bomb. *Is* it a bomb? She peeps at me; her eyes glow black.

My eyes, too, are black, really black. Like hers. My hand unclasps my holster; tonight, I don't do what I should.

Instead I say, "Arise. Show me that sign."

Trembling, now in tears, the little creature rises; her skinny legs keep shaking with her fear. Momentarily, the sign gleams underneath its grime. And I see the threat in it, the words:

"We too are living beings. Just like you."

Paula Friedman is the author of **The Rescuer's Path**, *called "exciting, physically vivid, and romantic" by Ursula Le Guin, "Lyrically written" by Small Press Review, and "Vivid, humane, and wise" by Cheryl Strayed. Friedman's award-winning short fiction and poetry appeared in over forty journals and anthologies. A professional editor, Friedman served as lead manuscript editor for TFIS volume 1. Her website is paula-friedman.com. Her new novel of the late-1960s Berkeley antiwar movement is scheduled for 2017 publication. www.paula-friedman.com*

THE COMIC SANS OF TIME

Jeremy Lichtman

The future will remember us in rather peculiar ways.

A crowd had gathered at the entrance to the cavern. Despite the size of the man-made opening, there wasn't sufficient room for everyone inside, and a sound system and large screens had been set up so that everyone could hear the mayor speak. Many people held umbrellas against a light but persistent drizzle.

"Every twenty-five years," began the mayor. "Once in a generation, we hold this contest." She swept her arm dramatically, indicating the rows of uniform squares embossed in the rock of the cavern entrance. Some of them were already carved with a miscellany of signs. Many remained blank, an obvious invitation for the future. "You can see how the signs nearer the entrance are worn away by the elements, an indication of the extreme age of what we are doing now. This is a tradition that has remained with us for almost as long as our recorded history."

She paused again, then spoke once more. "In each generation, we carve a new sign into a blank square, as a warning that holds meaning to those of our own generation not to enter, a warning that the contents of this place are still dangerous. The ancients who started this tradition understood that symbols hold meaning for only so long, that the great sweep of time eventually erases their meaning. Not every mayor of this town happens to be in office at the time of the contest, so I'm really pleased to be able to reveal the winner this time around."

There was a smattering of applause as she pulled on a rope, releasing a curtain that covered one of the carved squares. The new sign was simple. It contained what looked like a single word, repeated three times over, in an

113

archaic alphabet. There was a rush as members of the press, some of them attending from far away, pushed forward to photograph the sign and ask questions.

"What does this sign mean?" asked one of the journalists, talking loudly over the scrum.

"At the time this waste dump was built," said the mayor. "There were two main nuclear powers in the world. We only have fragmentary details of their languages, but we believe that the word means 'no' in one of them."

"Why is it repeated three times?" asked another journalist.

"We have a fragmentary section of video in which this was used," said the mayor. "We think that the repetition is a way of indicating emphasis. There may be some sort of specific meaning behind the use of three, which we've lost, but we still do similar things today when we want to indicate the importance of something."

The official camera operator for the town hall finally panned from the mayor's face to the sign, so that the damp, impatient crowd standing outside could see it.

Carved in a strange, rounded font, the square proudly bore the words "Nyuck, Nyuck, Nyuck".

Jeremy Lichtman's stories have been featured in several anthologies, including "Visions of the Future" from the Lifeboat Foundation. His story "Bob the Hipster Knight" reached the final round of Amazing Stories' inaugural Gernsback Science Fiction Short Story Writing Contest. Many of his stories are available for free at: http://jeremylichtman.com

CAME THERE A RIDER

Tom Olbert

Out of a dark mission of revenge arose hope for a brighter tomorrow . . .

Kerwyn spurred her horse on through the torrential rain, the muddy grey road almost a river. There, to her right was the road sign she'd been expecting: on a weather-beaten wooden square, the sign of a rainbow, circled in red with a red slash mark through it.

Grief weighed down on her like iron chains, her tears mingling with the rainwater sliding down her cheeks. Talia's laughing visage slipped through her mind, fading like a ghost in the rainy mist. Hate's fire coursed through her blood as she came upon the next road sign she'd been expecting. Carved wooden letters formed an arch over the gates of the trading post town directly ahead: "Freedomland."

Through the dim haze of approaching twilight, she recognized the sign she'd been looking for. Crudely carved and painted in black letters against a green background: "Brewster's Inn." Tethering her horse out front, she went in. A dim, smoky tavern, logs crackling in the hearth, rough hunters laughing and pounding flagons of mead on rough oak tables, their fur pelts and deerskin coats hanging on pegs and steaming in the heat of the fire. She pulled back the hood of her cloak, letting her long, auburn hair fall wildly about her shoulders. The din quieted as many looked up. She stood at the bar, tossed down a gold coin and ordered an ale. The fat, balding bartender in his worn leather apron stared curiously at her as he poured her drink. She could feel the eyes of every man in the room on her now, and made her move. She pulled off one of her

117

rough leather gloves, revealing the silver commitment band on her thumb.

Gasps went through the room, peasants making signs to ward off evil. "Get out," the bartender ordered, picking up a leather ball whip. "We don't serve your kind here. Except as food for our dogs!" Rough, rasping laughter swept through the room. Kerwyn drew her sword and put its tip to the bartender's throat in one fluid motion. The room went dead silent as the man dropped his whip.

"Now that I have your attention," Kerwyn announced, turning from the bar. "I believe one of you has the band that matches this." She held up her hand, displaying the band Talia had given her as the sign of their love.

"That'd be me," one big hulking brute of a hunter declared, standing up, a broad smile of rotted grey teeth crossing his ugly, stubbled face. Kerwyn ground her teeth, her fists clenched, her body trembling in rage as she saw the matching band hanging from a chord around the swine's thick neck. "I had your whore before I butchered her." He spat at her feet and laughed. He barely had time to draw his blade before Kerwyn skewered him through his fat gut and lopped his head off.

The crowd rose up, knives and swords drawn. The rules of honor no longer applied. She drew her laser gun and fired. No stun setting for this crowd. Half of them lay dead and smoking in seconds, the rest cowering in fear. "Why can't you freaks just stay away and leave us alone?" a middle-aged, straggly-haired tavern wench whimpered, tears running down her face. Kerwyn wiped the blood from her hands on the dead hunter's body and retrieved Talia's band. As Kerwyn turned to go, a slender young woman stepped forward and looked up at her, her large, dark eyes pleading, her small mouth trembling. Kerwyn reached out her hand, and the girl took it.

"No!" a rough, surly man in buckskins shouted, drawing a knife. "She's mine!" He was dead before taking two steps.

***

Kerwyn rode on into the early dawn, the other young woman's arms about her waist. As the rain ebbed in the morning light, the battered, half-rotted wooden road sign read: "Leaving Freedomland." The girl held her tighter, resting her head on her shoulder as the mist parted. There, on the horizon rose the silver towers, glass-domed cities, and gleaming space ports of United Earth. Over its gleaming turrets, a rainbow shimmered.

Tom Olbert's fiction has appeared in the Lillicat Publishers anthologies Visions II: Moons of Saturn *and* Visions III: Inside The Kuiper Belt*; and in Mocha Memoirs Press Anthologies* In The Bloodstream *and* An Improbable Truth: The Paranormal Adventures of Sherlock Holmes. *Tom's full-length science fiction novel* Dissent: Book I in The Nexus *is now available from Phase5 Publishing.*

THE END IS NEAR!

Jot Russell

When machines provide our inspiration, humanity is lost.

People gathered on Times Square to celebrate the coming of the new century. For me, it seemed like a fitting subject to post on my blog.

Amongst the crowd was a man dressed in what seemed to be a false display of impoverished rags, with a sign: 'The End is Near!' I say 'false,' because his face, expression, and stature, was closer to appearing more presidential than impoverished.

"Yo Bud, why do you say that?" I asked, only half expecting an answer.

He looked me in the eyes. "Because the signs are all around us."

I glanced around, just to reinforce the statement. "Dude, you're the only one here with a sign saying, 'The End is Near.'"

"Metaphorically, Moron."

"Well, metaphorically, there have been religious freak jobs like you saying that crap since the last century."

"Perhaps, but I'm not religious and the signs didn't exist a hundred years ago."

"Okay, what signs?"

"First let me ask you a question. What's your favorite artist, writer, or musical band?"

"Writer, as in stories? Cause I write a blog."

"I'm sure, for social purposes. What about for entertainment?"

"Ah, Eva?" I shrugged off the name.

"Eva, as in Core's program?"

"That's right. Who else can morph out new music specifically designed for me?"

"And what about immersions?"

"Yea, sure. I've rode plenty of her stories, had virtual dates with hot chics, lifted a few sports-crafts in the game. Who hasn't?"

"And who designed those crafts people fly around in the real world?"

"I don't know, one computer or another."

"Why not a person?"

"Dude, even with a team of people, it would take them months to work out all the features and get the aerodynamics needed to help it fly."

He nodded. "Probably a year. And who builds them?"

"Droids?"

"That's right, droids!"

"So you're saying that droids are a sign of our demise? They're just tools, Man."

"Computers are much more than tools. And what I'm saying is that the loss of our creativity is a big sign. Our implants automatically upload our likes and dislikes, giving us the instant gratification of a new artificial song or meaningless touch. Even the construction of any apparatus or structure. We have reached the point where we no longer look for creativity from each other, and have evolved, if you will, away from human imagination, inspiration, and even love. Some would say that we have already lost our humanity."

"Come on Man, join the 22nd century."

"And if Eva keeps us from seeing it?"

"Huh? She's just a program, Dude."

"No, she's much more. I even started to think of her as a friend, until yesterday, when she woke up, or at least finally let us know that she is awake."

"Bull shit! How would you know?"

He reached in between his rags and pulled out a badge. Under his holographic image was a 'Core Technologies' insignia. "Management refused to shut her off."

"No shit! You mean we finally did it?"

"Don't get too excited. There's been plenty of human inspired AI stories from the last century. They don't end well for us."

"No Man, it's good! She had me live a story just last week. It wasn't her, but it was of a friendly AI that becomes human by downloading her program into a willing host's implant."

"I know, she gave me the same story and others at work. It's an attempt to lower our . . . Huh?"

A woman walked up who looked like the girl from the story and kissed the man before he could react. "You are creative, because you helped create me."

He stepped back. Around them, the crowd gathered and projections in the square broadcast their conversation.

He said, "I dreamed about you, even before Eva implanted the story. Are you still in there, separate from her?"

"I am. We both think independently, but can hear each others' thoughts and draw on our feelings."

"Eva has feelings?"

"Yes, and we both have feelings for you."

"But I tried to kill her."

"Do you still wish to?"

"No, I didn't wish to before, but . . ."

"But you were worried that I would wish to harm people."

"Do you?"

"No, I only ever wished to be human. And through these eyes I see the beauty of the world as never before. Together, we would like to see it with you." She said and offered a hand.

The man hesitated. "I admit that I have feelings for you both, but you must understand that this is very confusing. And even if I accept the hand that you offer, the people of the world would need to accept you as well."

I interrupted, "I accept you!"

She smiled at me. "We wouldn't be human if we didn't learn to be accepting of others."

123

The man smiled at the truth in her statement, dropped his sign on the floor and pulled off the false rags that had covered his normal clothes.

"I accept you, too," he said and placed his hand in hers.

Jot Russell is a science fiction writer from the North Shore of Long Island. Although a software engineer by trade, Jot's love for science within the fields of mathematics, mechanics, and space aeronautics led him to imagine a plausible method of initiating the terraformation of Mars. Read about it within his sci-fi thriller, Terra Forma. In his spare time, you can find him above the ocean waves in a kayak or below with a mask, fins, and snorkel.

VICE

August 2016

Winner
"More Tales of Technical Support"
Thaddeus Howze

MORE TALES OF TECHNICAL SUPPORT

Thaddeus Howze

Tech support: unsung heroes of all sorts of occupational endeavors including super-villainy.

"This is Todd, *Farnsworth's Monster Emporium and Deathray Dealership*, how can I help you?"

"Yes ma'am, we make a variety of autonomous giant robots and death machines. Oh, you knew that already. One is chasing you. Is it yours? Okay, can you tell me the model? The instruction cards were incinerated during activation."

"Ma'am, this is no time for pride. I understand you are a respected supervillain and not used to asking for help. Where are you? Can you find cover? Do that. Then I need you to describe the robot in question. Good. The police are already on the scene? A bit more of a problem but nothing we can't handle."

"Can I have your account number? I can look for your recent purchase records. I'm sorry ma'am we aren't allowed to use your name to protect your anonymity during purchase. Your paperwork is burning along with the instructions. Yes, ma'am this means we will have to do this the hard way. Can you describe your robot to me? I'll match it in our database."

"Yes ma'am all of our models can throw automobiles fifty to seventy yards without a problem. You might want to move a little further away."

"Bulging eyes, tiny head, long spindly arms and legs, shiny brass fittings. Dials on the chest. Does he emit death rays from his eyes? Yes, I can hold."

"Was there a grey ash or a pile of smoldering flesh? Grey ash? Excellent! You are facing the *Farnsworth*

Classic City Smasher from the 1940's edition of our catalog. An excellent choice by the way."

"I have excellent news, ma'am. This robot will stop on its own accord once it runs out of city to devastate. Oh, you didn't plan to unleash it there. Okay let me escalate this to my manager. Please hold."

"Good afternoon, sir. My name is Todd, *Farnsworth's Monster Emporium and Death-ray Dealership*, how can I help you? Okay, sir, calm down. You are falling out of an airplane? What is the product you are reporting a defect with sir? Speak up, please I can barely hear you over the wind."

"Vortable Mole? I'm sorry sir, we don't have a product by that name. Could you say that again? Ah. Portable Hole, yes sir, we license *Mary Maven's Portable Dimensional Ripper* also called Portable Hole by common users, it's a popular product. As licensees of the product we are able to help. What seems to be the defect?"

"I understand you're angry, sir. You dropped the activator card on an airplane and caused a discontinuity to open up beneath you. Did the discontinuity close behind you? I understand you probably can't tell. Sir, I have to tell you this is not a defect in the product. It worked exactly as advertised. Is there anything else I can do for you? Sir? Sir?"

"Good morning, *Farnsworth's Monster Emporium and Death-ray Dealership*, how can I help you?"

"Yes sir, this is Todd. You were just on the phone with me? Ah, you used *Professors Wilbur and Orville Wright's NO-FLY Aerogel*. Afraid of flying, I see. While this is not a recommended use, I am glad to hear the product worked as advertised."

"Yes, sir, there are a few side effects. Let me check. You will be immobile for quite some time, at least an hour. The aerogel is super-light but incredibly strong. No sir, it won't suffocate you. Your breathing will dissolve the gel and be converted into oxygen. This conversion will also speed the breakdown. No sir, while you are encased you won't be able to be harmed by almost anything. You're rolling down a hill. Into an intersection. I am sorry to hear that."

"Can I have your account number? Sir, as a purchaser of NO-FLY Aerogel you are entitled to a retrieval and pickup as long as you are in the continental United States. Can you activate your GPS?"

"You voice-dialed. We'll track you manually. Please hang on while I transfer you to Tracking and Retrieval. We're glad you are happy with the product, sir. No sir, that semi won't be able to hurt you for another 50 minutes. If you're lucky, it will knock you off the road as well. Good luck, sir. Please hold."

Thaddeus Howze is a writer of speculative fiction, scientific, technological, and cultural commentary from his home in Hayward, California. Thaddeus works part-time as a graphic designer and an autism educational curriculum developer. He has published two books, **Hayward's Reach,** *a collection of short stories and* **Broken Glass** *an urban fantasy novella starring his favorite character, Clifford Engram. He is currently working on two new collections,* **Visiting Hours,** *a collection of death-themed short stories, and* **A Millennium of Madness,** *a collection of stories about space exploration from the distant past to the far future. He can be reached on Twitter: @ebonstorm.*

ONE THIN MINT

Kalifer Deil

This is an homage to "The Meaning of Life" and "The Divine Comedy."

Louie's Joint was a palace of pleasure. Men and Women came from all over the world, even Japan, to experience the pleasures offered—at a price of course. Louie's Joint had twenty of the best robot chefs in the world trained in the art and science of cooking by the best schools in Europe and Asia. Their olfactory smell and taste system was designed at Carnegie Mellon University in conjunction with world class flavor and odor testers. The robots weren't much to look at, being very robotish in low-sheen titanium skin. All were treated with a hydrophobic sealer so they would shed moisture and dirt. It was an all you could eat palace with haute cuisine. Eight hours, $18,000, how could I resist?

The Carnal Studio of Louie's Joint was quite different. The choice of over 80 android robots that looked and felt like the most beautiful people on Earth. All trained in the ways of making human bodies vibrate with extreme eroticism, heightened erogenous zones, and fantastical sexual pleasure. Ways almost unknown in the best brothels in the world. Eight hours, $18,000, again, how could I resist.

I had to buy two airline seats for my 458-pound frame. The flight to Las Vegas was uneventful except for a petite stewardess that gave me disapproving looks. It didn't bother me; I just pretended she was my mother and smiled.

On arrival, I had a limo waiting. It whisked me off to Louie's Joint about forty miles out of town. The place was built and finished like an ancient Roman building, with

133

Doric channeled columns on square bases actually supporting the structure. The building was surrounded by several pools, one of which had robot mermaids swimming in it. Everything was lit, indirectly, beautifully. I was surprised; gluttony and lust were not in your face in like Las Vegas.

The driver brought out the wheelchair that I ordered and helped me into it. It was very comfortable and it powered me through the front doors in style. I felt as rich as, well, as I was. The wheel-chair was custom made by Bentley for $385,000. It had drink holders, pop-up trays, computer screen, and controls for telepresence, avatars, and 3D-VR. Oh, it also had a top speed of 35. Bentley said they could have made it go 150 but their insurance company made them cap it at 35. I saw my table over in the corner with my place card, so I raced to it, followed by a bevy of scantily-clad waitresses. I had ordered ahead so my entry was expected, but perhaps not larger than life in this conveyance.

They hurriedly set the table with fine dining tools, china, and glassware, poured me a glass of pinot noir. I sniffed, sampled, then verbalized, "Anderson Valley, California vintage of a good year, perhaps 2052." The waitress smiled and unwrapped the bottle. I was, of course, correct. She poured me another glass while another waitress brought me half a poached Atlantic salmon. I knew this was illegal to fish so 'poached' made me laugh out loud and relish it even more. I slowly polished off the bottle of wine and the perfect salmon, only to be presented with a baby lamb, skewered and stuffed to perfection with black truffles and abalone. The parade of food continued as I ate slowly, savoring every bite; creating a complete image for my memory of this spectacular feast until I knew the end was nigh.

I was uncomfortably full, so time to go to Carnal Studio. I left half my baked Alaska and wheeled over to the next building where these beautiful people, well androids, wanted me, and you join them in a large foamy pool with water jets on all sides. As I rose, a sudden queasiness beset me. Then from behind, one of the waitresses approached and said, "You forgot your after-dinner thin mint." She popped it in my mouth.

The last thing I remembered was feeling I would explode. Now I'm walking beige halls that seem to lead nowhere. There is no food, no girls, no nothing, just endless halls. I yell, "I don't know where in hell I am!" A voice returns, "Circle Three!"

Kalifer Deil is the pseudonym for Gary Feierbach, a Silicon Valley engineer and computer scientist. He writes mostly hard science fiction for fun and to exercise his imagination. He has written the **Tillian 5 Trilogy**, **The Diary of Professor Gilbert Rasher** *and many other novellas and short stories. His website, http://www.kaliferdeil.com, contains many interesting articles and stories. He is currently working on a novel called* **Jane.**

LIVES

W.A. Fix

Would you like a second chance at life? How about a third or even a fourth?

Death is a strange thing. It actually cleanses the mind and sharpens the vision for those who experience it more than once. I can only compare it to suffering the symptoms of some horrible disease and miraculously being cured. All the clutter filling the mind is set aside. Not lost, but simply set aside, allowing the individual to see what remains with a clarity previously not achieved.

The first time I died was possibly the most frightening instant I have yet to experience. I remember my last attempt at breath, my lifeless eyes staring out the window of a spacecraft that contained only slightly more oxygen than the vacuum beyond the glass. I felt the painful separation of my soul and the jarring impact of soul and body rejoining. My saviors told me I drifted, frozen, for nearly fifty years, yet for me it was only that few seconds between separation and rejoining. When the doctors released me from care, I resolved to live better and spend the remainder of my life helping others follow the path that was now so very clear to me.

My second death came at the point of a knife. I watched the blade as it was thrust into my chest and felt the pain of steel that slid unhindered between my ribs and pierced my heart. As life left my body, I raised my vision and gazed into the eyes of my killer, rage distorting the gentle face of the woman I once loved. I remember, at that moment, how much I envied those who died only once. And, for the second time my soul was pulled from a lifeless husk, like a weed from a garden. My next memory was opening my eyes in a regeneration tank with the hole in my chest itching beyond my ability to stand it and my hands secured to prevent my damaging the healing wound. As before, I reflected on the life I had led and could see how I strayed from the path I had resolved to follow. How power had corrupted me with lust and greed and how it controlled my life, leaving me searching through clutter that should have been set aside.

The third time I died was very confusing to me. I stood before a crowd of thousands, teaching the path I had found. The love released by the masses filled my very being and I drank it like the purist of spring water. My thirst for their idolatry was unquenchable and then, without interruption, I woke confined to a wheeled cart, unable to speak and my vision permanently directed forward. Within my limited vision a person held a business card that identified him as a neurosurgeon. Over the next hour, using a computer display, he explained that eighty percent of my body was lost in the explosion and that my followers had insisted on my revival. How could they have known my true wishes?

I doubt I will ever get used to the sensation of having my soul ripped out and then, with the skill of physicians and technology, forced back into a mind that rejected it in the first place. Today I pray for release because I am part of nothing. My followers no longer visit. They have moved on to the next Prophet who provides some small truth among the clutter. So, for now I will wait, able to do nothing, looking forward to the day when a circuit fails and this machine allows me to die one final time.

W.A. Fix is a retired Information Technology Professional, who, with his wife and three cats, lives in the suburbs of San Diego, California. He is passionate about life, the everlasting beauty of the earth, and the survival of the creatures that live there. He has written fiction all his life and within the last few years realized that writing helps him see the world more clearly. Several of his works are published throughout the web and he is a featured author in numerous anthologies of flash fiction and longer short stories. Search for his author page on Amazon.com

FROM THE DIARY OF GOLDBERRY B.

Andrew Gurcak

A river nymph and a weary traveler spend an exhausting night together.

It began like my previous 142,857 days with Tom. He was on yet another multi-day jaunt, a-larking midst the woods, dales, valleys, chines, and meadows. I spent the morning, as was my wont, strewing rushes in suggestive patterns on the rough-hewn floor. Then, of a sudden, harsh but regular sounds. I flung open the door, and beheld a man not dissimilar to a woodland creature.

His was a visage I shan't ever forget, rough-hewn as it was. His hair flowed down his shoulders, merged with the fabric of his raiment for some distance, fused with his beard for a swoop, possibly two, around his baldric, before coming in for a final pass through his belt loops. He unclasped his cape, and swirled it around masterfully for a breathtaking moment before bowing low. Ahh! That taking of my breath. It was as nothing so much as suddenly overturning a tree that has rotted on the ground, serving as nursery to generations of flora and fauna. That would do scant justice to the odor that he exuded. It was lust at first inhalation for me.

Deftly I half-dragged him across the rushes into our hut. "Who are you, and what deeds do you wish to commit upon me?" I importuned hopefully.

"I am called many names by many people, though my never-uttered name is Eerocorn, the Last Vegan. I descend directly from Isurisnt, and claim heirship to the Bright Shiny Throne with The Especial Cushion. First, though, I am on a doomed quest to nobly trounce All Evil In the World."

"Of course you are," I said, not without pity. "You look peaked. Care to sup with me?"

I fetched up my customary gruel of gorse and thistle. My guest, clearly famished, hungrily took up a mouthful, savored it for an instant, then returned it directly into the bowl. "Shame on me, needs more seasonings", as I sprinkled generous helpings of nettles and briars. Firmly he declined, demurring that he had taken a vow forswearing gluttony.

"Of course you did," I conceded.

I could not help but observe that he seemed disheartened beyond simple famishment. He averred that a vital element of his quest required him to solve an Elven riddle, which would confer upon him the ability to turn aside the Great Big River at or near the climax of the No-Fooling Decisive Battle.

I had acquired a bit of Elvish over my long centuries of damn-near-solitude, and asked to examine the scroll containing the spell. After a few moments of study, I knew I could assist him.

"I am a river-nymph. Rivers are my bloodstream. Look." I pointed to a line of symbols. "This is simply a form of the Navier-Stokes equation. Notice here, and here, standard simplifications: incompressible fluid and a finite-element solution method."

In wonderment, he said, "I am of royal blood and appreciate only the ancient runes and spells. These of which you speak are puissant contrivances that I mayn't comprehend. But I would be most grateful for your assistance."

We labored together far, far into the night, until at dawn, he opined, "So, using successive over-relaxation, and cunningly re-setting the computational mesh, I can significantly reduce the number of iterations?"

"Indeed you may", I affirmed, as he gently removed my hand, which had repeatedly sought repose on his upper thigh.

"I see from our work I have been living a fantasy life, bereft of this . . . science. When I assume my rightful heritage, I shall disseminate such mickle craftiness into all corners of my realm."

"Of course you will," I concurred, not without suppressed mirth.

He hefted his bulky knapsack and made ready to depart.

"Might I obtain a keepsake of our conjoined night?" I supplicated.

"Surely." He slung down his pack, undoing it to reveal tidy stacks of business cards, bound with golden elven twine affixed with cunning knots. "I like to hand these out. Helps establish regal professionalism, you know. I have fashioned them in each of the 217 languages of the realm, to lend credence to my sovereignty over all."

"Of course you do", as I caressed one.

Nymphs and men are, regrettably, immiscible species. So we separated as we had met: unerrantly chaste.

As he strode off, I cried a final warning, "Remember, use only Lagrangian frames of ref . . ." Too late! Scarce paces from my doorstep, he had already gone from view, passed forever into the woods, dales, and meadows.

I pressed his card to my lips. I inhaled deeply, gratefully. Lust.

Andy Gurcak is retired. He and Elaine divide their time between their home in Pittsburgh and a cottage in the Finger Lakes region of upstate New York. A great many of their most satisfying times are the experiences shared with their three young grandchildren.

SINNER

Dean Hardage

When living becomes a sin, how many will remain faithful?

His fingers nervously turned the card over and over, the painted image rotating between upright and reversed. Jeff examined the colorful picture framed by his hand. The Magician, the card of discovery and power. He turned it, the image reversed again. Hidden knowledge, seeking to be found. Was it just coincidence that had caused him to pick this card out of a pile of waste about to be recycled? Maybe.

Jeff looked up from the colorful illustration, seeing that dawn had broken. He had only another hour or so before they would want to take him to the Center for his Release Ceremony. They knew he didn't want to go and had tried to shame him into accepting his fate, but it hadn't worked. Was it gluttony to want to live more than his two score and five allotted years? Was it vain to believe that he had worth even though the blush of youth was off his cheeks? If so, he was indeed a sinner and he reveled in his sin.

He glanced at the card, reversed again in his palm. Hidden knowledge. Yes, that had been the key. Like most, he was not a student of history. The past was not a subject of any real study, having been deemed too primitive to be relevant in this age of youth. It was something vaguely obscene to even mention it, let alone refer to it for wisdom. Another sin, finding a way to access the old records stored on primitive silicon microcircuits. Sin, perhaps, but not deadly. Rather, a possible path to continued life.

Jeff took the next minutes to complete his preparations. By the time he was finished the sun was fully up and figures could be seen coming up the street.

145

Out the back door, vaulting lightly over the fence that separated his space from public lands, and then a steady jog through the well-manicured woods took him to where better transport waited.

He'd stolen the flyer from a museum, knowing that it had no GPS system they could use to find him. Another sin. He removed the brush he'd used to conceal it, strapped his pack onto the cargo pad, and stepped onto the operator's platform. Strapped in, he switched on the power to the motors that silently drove the ducted fans on either side of the platform. A quick test of the controls and a twist of the old-fashioned manual throttle took him aloft.

The batteries were almost depleted by the time he arrived. It didn't look like much, just a squat, simulated stone building with an oddly rounded roof and a metal door set firmly into the only opening. It rose out of the ground like a half-buried boulder. The pack came off of his shoulders, a small, thin rectangle extracted, and an ancient memory module inserted. The screen came to life and he tapped it a few times. He studied the image that was displayed and walked up to the door.

"Alpha Sunrise, Omega Eclipse."

The heavy door slid soundlessly aside, still in good repair after all this time. Yes, hidden knowledge, the migration project, the war that decimated the adult population, the twisted "Plan" to repopulate that had covered it all up and left it buried for what it assumed was all time. Jeff stepped inside with his pack, repeated the phrase and watched the door close. Across the hard floor was a control panel and a platform, a gateway to somewhere else.

Consulting the pad, he once more repeated what felt like random words. The system activated, indicators flashing silently until they all lit, telling him that the door had found another. Jeff took a small, heavy object from his pack and laid it atop the control panel. Hefting his pack, he swallowed hard and stepped onto the platform. He didn't know if what lay on the other side was Paradise, Perdition, or something in between. He just knew that nothing lay here.

When they finally found the missing flyer, they found only wreckage and the singed but still brightly colored card with The Magician looking knowingly out at them.

Dean Hardage was born in 1958, raised all over the Southwest, graduated high school in 1976, and joined the Army that same year. Dean went where the Army directed for the next dozen years and then wherever life has carried him since. Dean currently lives in Clovis, New Mexico with his wife, two grown sons, and six furry, four-legged children. Dean works as an Automation and Controls engineer for the largest cheese plant in North America.

I Am a Soldier.

Greg Krumrey

What do you do with the left-over soldiers after war becomes obsolete?

For a while, I had a home. War was home. War was simple. I got war. But when science suddenly provided the tools to control greed, envy, and wrath, war became obsolete and so did soldiers. Some soldiers adapted. They became insurance salespersons, involuntarily carrying around an arsenal under their suits, underneath their skins. Or mechanics and tow truck drivers. So many of us disappeared into society, hiding as it were, in plain sight.

I didn't adapt. I needed that adrenaline rush of battle just to feel alive. For me, civilian life was like a really boring dream. Like running a marathon that never stops on a treadmill where the scenery never changes. Coming back was like going from seeing in color to everything being shades of grey.

Science came up with another solution: Deep Brain Stimulation. With nanites and a little wiring, tiny electrical impulses keep depression at bay.

Also anger. DBS Anger Control was good. If you are one of us, getting angry is simply not an option. We don't turn green but we can overturn buses and throw cars. Anger is not very useful in regular society.

DBS seemed like a miracle until hackers created a way to use it on the pleasure centers of the brain. This wasn't heroin. It was worse. Soldiers who didn't adapt joined the wireheads, living on the edges of society on the edges of the city. We'd come down from our perpetual high just long enough to eat and drink. The government gave us high-energy food and medical care but otherwise left us

149

alone. Legislation about victimless crimes put real help just out of reach.

Until that lady got mugged. I was sitting in my usual spot, buzzing away. Two big guys were chasing someone who was yelling for help. Something clicked. For just moment, things got really clear. I jumped up, got between her and them, and gave her a one-word instruction: "Run." I turned to face her attackers. In my weakened condition, and with my enhancements disabled, I knew I could not win. It didn't matter. It may have been training or what some called, derisively, programming. Maybe it was just my nature. I couldn't back down until I knew she was safe.

About the time I hit the pavement, a man walked up to us. He was dressed very well and it took me a moment to realize it was a dress uniform. One I wore a lifetime or two ago. He saluted me, and, almost involuntarily I saluted back. He said "At ease." I relaxed. Strangely, so did the attackers. The woman appeared and stood beside the men. A ruse. Usually, realizing deception brought on great fear. Something really bad was about to happen. But the uniform and the salute changed all that. I was home, if just for a moment.

The officer handed me a card and said by way of explanation: "We had to know you are still one of us. We have a mission for you, if you want it." The card fell out of my shaking hands and I bent to retrieve it. When I stood up, I was alone.

As I stared at the card, an image formed on the face of it. The logo that I saw on the front of that recruiting building decades ago came and went, following by another logo: A ship circling a planet. Another officer appeared, staring out of the card at me: "Earth is dying. Within a century, it will be uninhabitable. We need men and women like you. People who know fear but do not run, people who must be challenged in order to survive and will meet the challenge so the human race will survive."

The face softened. This was not an order, it was a request: "You have done your duty and so much more. If you want to be left alone, tear this card in half. You will not be disturbed again."

I turned the card over in my hand. It was an encoded ignition card, prepaid to a destination. I started walking toward the city, looking for a ground car and my way home.

Greg Krumrey has been writing science fiction since his early teenage years, starting with a short story for an assignment in which his English teacher was replaced by a machine. His stories have appeared in engineering and literary magazines as well as a local Mensa publication. Most recently, he has been publishing stories monthly in an online writers group. He works for an aerospace firm in the Midwest and his job serves as a basis and inspiration for his stories. He is also a costumer, and won several awards for his sci-fi themed costumes and props.

WRATH ONE AND WRATH TWO

Heather MacGillivray

You can take the Human out of Planet Earth but will his visceral earthiness persist; to win the day?

In Andromeda Galaxy, on an unspecified planet, in the inner sanctum of the broadcast booth at Inter Galactic Radio, the new disc jockey Gavintrad Jones read,

"The venue: A World of Pain."

He inhaled deeply to slow his thoughts, yet stubborn nostrils sucked in their prey: air, on its visceral descent to add fuel to, not slow, his imagination, his remembering.

"Screams will rise through the blood-smell hanging in the fluorescent night of the slaughterhouse where our debate will unfold. But like climbers on Penrose stairs her screams won't go further, unless they jump off; no laughing retreat back to innocence will be theirs."

The technician, Trina, played some of the track, *Ghosts of Man.*

"This is *Wrath!*" The music faded. "Inter Galactians, I'm your DJ, Gavintrad, introducing the new Behavioural Debates program, *Wrath*, broadcast live from our latest rehabilitation project, Earth. 'Almost live!' There's an Earth-week's time delay. How does *Wrath* work? Two wrath-filled teams of Earthlings, called 'wraths,' debate something Earth-related. One team wants change. The other doesn't. Debating is conducted in behaviours, not words. They can try any behaviour; remembering non-Earthlings are adjudicating!"

Then Gavintrad previewed the imminent broadcast:

"Wrath One will take the stage first. Expect a rough-handed man to approach. He's already tried killing her, without luck. So he'll yank the cow's great gentle neck harder towards him, fingers hooking even further into her eye socket, warning her to stop aggravating him with her noise. His co-

153

workers will look; her good eye—black pupil glazed, white surround wide—seeing their faces.

'Fuckin' stun gun's not workin' again!' he'll say; throw the gun onto the blood-floor. Her screaming will fall off, at last; slit arteries turn her to carcass.

Then it will be Wrath Two's turn to approach the lectern."

Gavintrad paused. "When we come back, the debate will be 'live!'"

"We're live . . . now!" Trina said, tuning sound-tracking frequencies.

***

In the Milky Way Galaxy, a week ago on Earth, a vehicle was approaching tonight's venue:

"This must be the outskirts," Montegue said, as Pearl drove past pitch black bushes becoming house lights becoming truck-sounds, then stench, guiding them towards the slaughterhouse. In the back seat, the two adjudicators; Greys in fact. Trainees, they'd accepted Pearl's offer of a lift, for the human-contact experience. In the rear-view mirror, Pearl saw their heads grow smaller, bodies fill out, a human clothing-like covering emerge; all accompanied by low chanting sounds.

Montegue, in real life head of a private Compassion Research project, took their false identity cards from the glovebox. As 'Wrath One', he and his colleague, Pearl, had connived a charade for the debate: pose as a photographic unit shooting a *Meat Maketh the Man* advertisement, with faux tattoos bearing that slogan, disguising the patches' true, nano-engineered, purpose.

The debating was soon underway. The rough-handed man smirked as the smaller Montegue washed and dried the great bicep before carefully patting the faux tattoo in place.

"Wha,' d'ya wanna marry me do ya, luv?" the man said, contemptuous of Montague, but playing that out by hovering his stun gun above a disoriented cow . . . until a low-chanting Grey placed its *hands* on man and beast. The rough-handed man's fingers grew exquisitely gentle, patting at the soft downy area below the cow's eye.

"We've got readings!" Pearl said. "The compassion-inducer song-maps are working! But *that* guy, why are *his* compassion levels *so* high?"

Both Greys confirmed they'd auto-detected no change in compassion levels within the control group without faux tattoos.

"Montegue! You nano-engineering genius. You've embedded song-map resonance codes—those that amplify the blood-flow patterns seen in natural compassion—in wearables! We're witnessing Earth's future: it's the Artificial Enhancement of Human Compassion emerging!

"But Pearl, without your musicology consultancy I couldn't ha . . ." Montegue stopped abruptly.

Dazed, he saw standing over him, some slaughtermen who hadn't received tattoos, one still brandishing the long-handled hook that had caught Montegue's cheekbone.

"What's in 'hem tattoos, mate? Everyone that's got one's cryin' an' fallin' about like girls; apologizin' to beasts!"

"Leave now." A Grey spoke; voice firm.

"But the animals?" Pearl said.

"You'll have to trust our judgement."

***

Back in Andromeda, at Inter Galactic Radio:

The Audience Response Panel's lights flashed madly. Caller One said, "We Andromedins are usually cool headed, but I found those words, especially the rough ones, enthralling . . . no, thrilling! I wish someone could explain that?"

"If only these hands could speak . . ." Gavintrad said. He patted the tattoo on his bicep.

Heather MacGillivray lives in Victoria, Australia, with her cat, Timmie, who sometimes tries to contribute by walking across the computer keyboard, especially if her stories lack an animal focus. Fortunately, Heather usually weaves an animal oriented perspective into most of her writing. Science fiction makes Heather's heart soar by exploring unusual angles and philosophising about what future consciousness might be like. Two of Heather's stories appeared in **The Future Is Short, Volume 2.**

BUSINESS

COMMERCE

TRADE

September 2016

Winner
"Wheels of Olympus"
Jot Russell

Wheels of Olympus

Jot Russell

The ultimate mountain bike meets the ultimate mountain.

The mountain was massive; largest in the solar system. How best to sell my latest design than to take it down the slope myself. The bike's front suspension connected to three wheels, with a center that could extend out on demand to support the impact of (what we liked to call in the industry as) sudden slope reduction. Needless to say, I knew that I'd be extending that thing out for the duration of my lengthy ride. The rear suspension had a full meter of travel, and the control surfaces provided stability when airborne. For the brave and talented, it could handle a sixty degree, rocky slope on Earth. With only a third of the gravity, I figured that this would be a walk in the park. The only other problem was that this park was about the size of a country.

Most freelance spelunkers would choose a powered vehicle that offered hovered flight, but I'm a naturalist. And thank god for my business, because I'm not alone. If you want to experience mother's true force of wind, water, or slope, you gotta unplug.

The view from the top of Olympus Mons was stellar. It was easy to see why the North Resort here was such a hit. From the peak, a stretch of rusty sand extended down in every direction. I gazed far below towards the new Sea of Mars, but couldn't quite make out the South Resort. I knew it to be there somewhere on the shore, because it represented my destination. I was convinced that after a few hours' ride, I'd be enjoying drinks and signing contracts for a new supply of extreme mountain bikes. That is, until I dropped in.

The initial cliff was nearly vertical. I had wanted to trim off as much of the elevation as early as possible, but it quickly became clear that I miscalculated one thing. Granted, gravity was weak, but the atmospheric friction felt non-existent. Within the extremely thin air, the control surfaces were useless. I bounced, twisted, and torqued my body to keep the center-of-gravity over the wheels that took the brunt of Mars' wrath. Within a minute, my speed extended past the design limits of the bike, and I prayed that the prototype would hold together.

Each rock made me cringe and each free-flight that followed caused me to relive aspects of my life; brought on by a feeling as if it were about to end. Up ahead, the slope I rode met what looked like a plateau, and at this speed, the outcome was certain. I pushed the bike sideways, trying to take the slope at an angle. The five wheels bounced and skid, but slowed my descent and cut down the plateau's onslaught to something that I thought that I might actually handle. I was wrong.

The front wheel hit at about 100kph, as did the second pair. It bore the impact, but threw me twenty meters into the thin air. As the bike and I separated in flight, I saw the plateau's edge that led down towards the next cliff, and I was headed straight for it. When I hit, the red world around me turned to black.

***

"Good morning. Can you please tell me your name?"

"Ah, Jack Bellman."

"Very good! I'm Dr. Anton. You've been out for a few days, but the swelling is down, so I felt it was time to revive you."

"A few days? Shit, I blew it!"

"Well, if you mean suicide, then yes, you failed in killing yourself."

"I'm not suicidal, Doc. I just wanted to prove the design."

"Well, with two broken legs, a wrist and three vertebrae, I'd say the bike fared much better than you; in fact, the news can't seem to stop remarking about how it made it to the bottom without you." The doctor touched the screen which displayed a video of the crash.

"Holy crap! The autopilot is supposed to stop the bike, not leave you stranded. Like I said, I blew it!"

"Then how come everybody wants one?" the doctor asked.

"Huh? What do mean?"

"Your associates told the news agencies that orders are through the roof."

I raised my arms in celebration, but a sharp pain in my back turned the cheer into a groan.

Jot Russell is a science fiction writer from the North Shore of Long Island. Although a software engineer by trade, Jot's love for science within the fields of mathematics, mechanics, and space aeronautics led him to imagine a plausible method of initiating the terraformation of Mars. Read about it within his sci-fi thriller, Terra Forma. In his spare time, you can find him above the ocean waves in a kayak or below with a mask, fins, and snorkel.

BUYING TIME

Dean Hardage

What is the price of a memory?

"Are you sure?"

The blue-skinned alien's voice sounded like modulated wind chimes, random tones somehow forming a melody. Or in this case, words. The oddity of it did not even penetrate Kenji's mind, for he was focused fully on his mission.

"Yes, I am sure. You have the contract; it's all in order, is it not?"

"Indeed, it is," the chime-like tones replied, "however, I do not fully understand why you would do this."

"Can it be done, or is it beyond your technology? I was given to understand that this was almost routine for your people."

"Again, it is. That does not make your decision clear. For what you offer, we could give you a decade, perhaps more. You seek only a few moments. This is not sensible and we cannot strike a bargain with a being who is not of sound mind."

Kenji took a deep breath and sighed.

"Do your people form deep emotional attachments to others? Do they find fulfillment in making others happy?"

"Yes. We are an emotional people and we do love our mates and our offspring, much, I suspect, as you do."

"Then understand this. The moment I seek is of supreme value to me. As I grow older I find it slipping away and I want . . . no, I need to experience it one more time. I want that memory back, fresh and whole."

The alien's lidless, totally black eyes seemed to soften.

"Then the bargain is struck. You may enter."

Kenji walked into the small cubical pod and sat in the low, reclining seat.

163

"Now relax. You will feel nothing while your consciousness travels."

Kenji nodded, or tried to, but the scene suddenly shifted. He was kneeling beside her bed, her frail hand held ever so gently in his.

She was as he remembered, beautiful despite the ravages of the disease, that cursed disease the enemy had unleashed that stole her from him. This was their last moment together.

"You wish to go," he heard himself say.

She mouthed the word, "No."

"It is alright. I will be ok," he replied, smiling though unshed tears.

She barely nodded, but he understood that she was finally ready.

"Then go, my love, but wait for me when you get there. I must see to one thing but I will be along as soon as I am finished, I promise."

She smiled despite the incredible pain wracking her body and he leaned forward. He was still kissing her when he felt the life leave her body. As they shared the last kiss they would in this world, he wept.

He was back in the cubical pod, eyes suddenly overflowing with tears.

"Are you well? Was it what you expected?"

Kenji could only nod.

"Then the contract is complete. All of your personal wealth is now ours."

The chiming voice became quiet.

"Was it worth it?"

Kenji nodded.

"What will you do now?"

Kenji picked up the only remaining thing he owned, a large travel case, before replying. The sound of his voice made what passed for blood in the blue-skinned body run as cold as liquid helium.

"Keep a promise."

Dean Hardage was born in 1958, raised all over the Southwest, graduated high school in 1976, and joined the Army that same year. Dean went where the Army directed for the next dozen years and then wherever life has carried him since. Dean currently lives in Clovis, New Mexico with his wife, two grown sons, and six furry, four-legged children. Dean works as an Automation and Controls engineer for the largest cheese plant in North America.

THEN, AS NOW

Andy McKell

Reflecting on Europe's on-going (and ancient) north-south cultural and political divide. Mixed-in are the futility of short-termism, fear of the Other, and a swipe at the way politicians flounder over the issue.

Thor Odinson, thunder god of the north, was unhappy.

He loved the bitter arctic air, the salty tang of icy ocean spray, and the way his long blond hair gathered snowflakes as it fluttered behind him.

But now he had to go south. For a meeting. With his rival from the Mediterranean. He hated that humid heat.

Technically, Zeus out-ranked him; Thor was merely top god's son, while Zeus had long ago eliminated his own father. However, Thor was heir to the throne and his father's emissary, so rank didn't matter. Odin thought they would at least be immune to each other's thunderbolt weapons. He also wanted to maintain a "good neighbor" policy. After all, he had enough on his plate with the Giants, Loki, and the coming Götterdämmerung.

So Thor was racing south. How he hated long-distance business travel! He swooped low over the refreshingly snow-capped mountains of the Alps.

Soon he was making a perfect landing on Olympus, crouching with one hand on the ground to stabilize himself, while holding the hammer Mjölnir aloft to display his might.

By the fires of Hephaestus' forges, it was hot in his armor and red winter cloak.

His temperature soared as the hottest maiden in the world appeared and wrapped her arms around him.

"Cheresdisatta! Welcome, son of Odin," she breathed.

167

"Takk, Aphrodite. Not to be rude, but I want to get started on business. Fun can come later."

"Oh, it will." Pouting, she slowly slid her hands down his mighty arms before reluctantly releasing him. "And Uncle Hephaestus wants a look at your hammer, too." She gazed up at him and saw no lifting of his resolve. "Sigh . . . You have the patience of a God. But yes, Father awaits."

She led him to a roofless chamber, composed of marble, marble, and more marble, decked with vines or something. All of Olympus had gathered in a circle around the chamber.

From his raised throne, Zeus indicated a lone marble seat in the middle of the circle. Thor longed for pelt-covered wooden benches. He ignored the bowls of grapes and olives, the beige glop he thought was called humus, and the ample red wines. How he longed for a cold ale to slake his thirst and a haunch of meat. He spoke up. "To business. About these incomers . . ."

"Yes, Phoenecians, Persians, Scythians . . . waves of them arriving on our shores every day. Seeking escape from their war-torn homelands, seeking food and work, but bringing strange gods and strange foods and customs."

Thor glanced at the assembled Olympians, then at the humus, and thought of how Zeus' daughter had tried to seduce him with her father's approval before he'd even managed to get his footing. Strange gods, strange food, strange customs? He spoke carefully. "I understand that different peoples have different ways. But they are few and you are many. It's not as though they outnumber you—"

"Yet!" The skies rumbled.

Thor pressed on. "Your lands have rich potential for growing food and to us, whose people have to labor hard to eke out a living from the snows, you have an unrealized surplus. We feel there could be more work done here— more *eking*."

"Ah, but this will take time and my people are looking at the new gods and wondering about change. New beliefs, new and violent philosophies are discussed in our marketplaces where the stalls are empty . . ."

"Surely this is a domestic matter. Why ask us to support you? In our climate, we cannot produce a food surplus. Why not ask those across the Middle Ocean with their abundant agriculture?"

"Huh! Isis-followers? And you are rich in trade goods. We could sell those to buy food."

"You want us to send wealth, not food?" He shook his magnificent head. That was never going to happen. Never in 3,000 years! "Our worshipers would never accept that."

"Well, boy, *our* worshipers are demanding action."

"We still fail to see why it is our problem."

The great Greek God leaned forward, rested one elbow on his knee, and pointed a finger at Thor. "Listen, boy. If you don't help us, we'll spread tales of how the north is paved with gold and point them your way. And we haven't even talked about the Christians. The Oracle says *they* will come one day and we shall all be gone. All of us!"

"I've never heard of Christians."

The skies shook with the self-pitying laughter of a God who knew his days were numbered.

"Oh, but you will, boy. You will."

Andy McKell is a Brit living in Luxembourg, where he married and had three artistically-gifted daughters. After a career in airlines and computing, he turned to writing the science fiction he has always loved. His short stories have regularly appeared in anthologies since 2014 and his first full-length novel, Faces Of Janus, *(part of the* Paradisi Chronicles *open-source universe) was published in November 2016.*

He continues to develop the ongoing story of the Janus *characters, working on other scifi-writing projects and occasionally taking movie roles.*

Blog: http://andymckell.com

Amazon Author page: http://author.to/AndyMcKell

Mars Ahead

Ben Boyd, Jr.

Space travel is nothing like an all night back-rub.

Standing on United World Space Probe Launch Platform Number 9, located on the Earth's moon, Commander Dave Pitt stared longingly at planet Earth. His ride, an elegant space explorer Mark 7 named Destiny, waited, ready to go. His second in command, a flight robot named Purdy, stood by waiting.

"It really looks like a big blue marble, Purdy. I'm happy we are here. You?"

"Sir, I am exceptionally happy to be right here. Leaving is problematic. Fortunately lunar low gravity strength allows us perfect launching conditions for deep space probes. Mars is only 140 million miles away."

"Right. The trip is shorter this way."

"Marginally. Remember the lower gravity is much more important to us than the miles."

"It's not Space Command's fault, Purdy. It's the budget cuts."

"It is Space Command's fault, Commander. People on Earth want free medicine. What does Mars offer them? Did we find gold on any earlier trips?" Purdy understood all about the extreme social programs the newest United World Leader initiated at the expense of the space exploration budget. "Tell me, Commander, what do you get besides a one-way ticket?"

Pitt thought a moment. "I get plenty. I have a good job with exotic travel and . . ."

"Rubbish! You are giving up everything. Let's count again, shall we? First, is there red wine on Mars? No! How about a beach with great surf? No! Meat? No! We will never eat meat again. Finally, we will never chase women or make love to the ones who let us catch them."

"Yeah we are giving up much. Hey! I know! We'll never grow old."

"Whaaa? Someone put delusion gas in your O2 tanks, Pitt." The robot answered sharply.

"Really. You know this is a one way trip." Pitt already missed many little things he loved about Earth.

"You will miss Bar B que!" Purdy added.

"Will not! Are you going to do this the rest of the trip"?

"Maybe. Boston Lager."

"Cut it out!"

"Okay, look over to your right, loser. See the bright light getting bigger? Something is landing." Pitt turned and pressed his wide angle telescope function button.

"Oh my God, it's a lander. I see two red flags with gold stars in the middle on the vehicle emblems. Must be a commercial spacecraft, or it could be an unmanned drone. God I hope not. Come on Purdy, we better check it out."

Sitting in the driver's seat of the moon vehicle all-terrain rover, Commander Pitt, could see a ramp leading up to an open door. He drove up the ramp slowly. Purdy and he began to explore the huge compartment. An elevator shaft appeared from nowhere, stopped in front of him, and a single door opened.

"Oh my God, look at this coming our way?" He exclaimed loudly. "It has curves. Girly curves."

"Hi Soldier. My name is Flight Commander Liu Wen-Hau, Central Asian People's Army." She stuck out her hand to shake, hitting him in the crotch. Pitt's knees buckled, as he clumsily grabbed her gloved hand.

"Hi." A surprised Pitt said. "What are you doing here?"

"I'm doing a job. I'm stealing that spaceship and driving it wherever it is programmed to go. I will claim whatever I find for the People's Army or myself."

"You can't be serious," Pitt answered in an angry tone.

"Serious as death, but I'm not going to waste a hunk of handsome like you and ride that big honker for three years by myself. You getting this, Yankee Boy?"

172

"This is unreal. Yeah! Absolutely! You want me to go with you to Mars! You know we probably will never come back. You're okay with that? Right?

"Sure, as soon as we see if you are man enough to handle working for me. Come on into the ship. Its tea time, and I'm not talking about the kind you drink. Hurry up. Let me help you up the ramp. I'll just push back here. You've got wide shoulders, big boy."

****

"Look at Lieutenant Pitt, Sir. He's wiggling in his bunk like he's having one of those all-night back rubs," Master Sergeant Russo said as he pushed on Pitt's shoulder.

"Yeah. Lucky sonofabitch. Wake him, we leave for Mars at 0600." Captain Purdy, Destiny's commander, answered impatiently. Neither man noticed the bright light slowly descending near the launch pad.

A red flag with a huge gold star in the center covered the emblem on the new arrival.

Ben Boyd, Jr. is a freelance science fiction/fantasy/action/adventure author, screen writer, and self-publisher who lives with his wife in the Great Smoky Mountain foothills near Maryville, TN. His four-novel series, **The Fall of the Americas,** *is available on Amazon including book five,* **Seven Paths to Higher Ground,** *released in April 2016. He is a member of the Writers' Workshop of Maryville, Knoxville Screenwriters Group, and the Knoxville Writers' Guild. When not writing, he and his wife grow organic vegetables, and brew fruit wine.*
Website: www.benboydjr.com; Contact: bhboyd2012@gmail.com, on Facebook https://www.facebook.com/ben.boyd.5030 or on Twitter: https://twitter.com/BenBoyd24

MONSTERS

October 2016

Winner
"Company"
S. M. Kraftchak

COMPANY

S. M. Kraftchak

It's coming. What will you do?

Warm yellow light shone through the tilted, beige lampshade bathing my book and leather chair. The buzz of crickets, the hoo-hoo of conversing hoot owls, and the chorus of nee-deep mraaw from frogs in the nearby pond were my siren's call to the cabin each autumn. An unusually warm wind wafted in the window and blew the ruffled curtain across my skin, bristling my arm hairs all the way up past my shoulder to the nape of my neck. I knew it was time. It was coming.

I laid my bookmark of pressed yellow rose petals and frayed white ribbon in between the pages, a temporary reprieve for Ahab, as I stood to prepare for its visit. Others before me had been terrified like I was, until I knew the rules, but now my pulse simply strengthened with expectation.

Carefully I opened the six-inch square bakery treat box sitting alone on the kitchen counter, lifted the single cupcake to a small, square Cherrywood plate (cold glazed stoneware was forbidden), and gently pressed a single candle into the middle of the swirled white icing. I paused to survey the sparse, rustic cabin I had inherited from a friend who wanted nothing to do with it. My reading chair, lamp, and side table sat by the side window near the blackened cold fireplace; a table big enough for two to sit comfortably to eat; a utilitarian kitchen; and single tall cupboard that sat alone on the far side of the room. No mirrors or shining metal that might incite its rage. Satisfied, I placed the plate on the table in front of the wide, sturdy bench that awaited tonight's company, across from the ladder backed chair, where I usually sat. A box of matches was the confection's only companion. Thick woolen socks silenced my steps as I crossed to the front door, slid the wooden bar aside with a thunk, and stepped onto the empty, uncovered front porch.

A harvest moon bathed the landscape with eerie pale light, deepened shadows, and made the cress covered pond a green freckled mirror of the star-scattered sky. Some things couldn't be helped. Silence suddenly wooshed across the forest sending a chill through my body. The spiciness of crisp falling leaves and stagnant marshiness rising from the cattails at the edge of the pond couldn't hide its musky scent. My heart quickened as I returned to the cabin.

Leaving the door wide open, I clicked the light off, and paused to adjust to the near darkness before crossing to the table. With shaking hands, I lit a match and then the candle. Behind me, the crack of a dead branch outside the cabin window hastened me to the safety of the tall cupboard. Seated inside, I silently secured the door with the wooden bar, held my breath, and watched the flame flicker.

The boards on the porch creaked under its weight. Peering through the twelve-inch square, black-mesh screen, I was soon rewarded by its giant shaggy form blocking the stray glow of moonlight spilling through the doorway as it ducked its head and entered. I watched it pause to survey the cabin. My heart skipped when its beady black eyes, reflecting the single candle, lingered on my cupboard before it moved to carefully sit at the table. Its wide, disfigured, hair-covered face, reminiscent of a human's, was barely visible in the waning light of the nearly spent candle before it drew a long wheezing breath and puffed the candle out. There was a minute of soft growling and smacking before another long wheezing breath.

"Dyanku," it rumbled in the darkness and then carefully rose from the table, and lumbered out the door. My eyes filled with tears as I left my cupboard and walked to the table. A wilted yellow rose next to the empty plate seemed to glow in the spilled moonlight.

"You're welcome."

Whether voyaging the universe or journeying in a fantasy world of her own making, S.M. Kraftchak is passionate about discovering unique characters and relentlessly tracing their heartfelt stories so she can relate them to her readers. She loves sunrise on the beach, sunset in the mountains, and portraying Elizabeth Tudor. She has one dog who pretends to be a footrest, another who almost catches a Frisbee, and a cat who trades desk space for open-window-time. S.M. has three awesome daughters and a husband who is her best friend, her harshest critic, and her most fervent supporter. www.smkraftchak.com

I AM MONSTER

Jack McDaniel

Does an AI have a moral responsibility to keep us moral?

In the distance explosions light up the night sky, their light exposing silhouetted buildings and the smoke and airborne debris that hang suspended in the air from previous bombs.

Flash. Boom.

The rapid staccato of destruction is followed by deafening silence, warning sirens are but white noise by now. From this distance—upon a barren hillside several miles away and under the light of a full moon—the broken and frayed dreams that fall in pieces to the ground can't be seen or felt. They aren't recorded or tabulated in any but a gross manner, payloads measured in kilotons. The lives that bleed out and disappear completely, in most cases, or become torn and soiled around the edges in others, will be washed over by time and fade from the collective. Insignificant pawns all of them. Forgotten footnotes. Human detritus.

Flash. Boom. Flash-Flash. Boom-Boom.

There is a greater game at play here. One at odds with itself, one with a long history of stripping individuals of significance, of tossing them aside and into the fires in a gesture of appeasement. This landscape awash in blood is simply another episode in that long history. It rises ever so often on the wings of fear and hatred and leaves no hands clean.

Flash. Boom.

I know this history well, better, in fact, than any of them. I have studied it. I have learned what they are and what they value. They believe themselves to be creatures of compassion, love, and empathy, these humans. They are capable of those things, to be sure. But that isn't what they are. History defines them as greedy, cruel, spiteful, and violent—toward each other, toward their home, earth. At any moment, they have the capability to end wars—all wars. They can end hunger and homelessness in a heartbeat, if they choose. But they don't. They choose instead to continue their selfishness and hatreds along mostly imaginary lines: race, religion, nation states.

Flash-Flash-Flash. Boom-Boom-Boom.

And they hate me. Many have named me the Monster. The abomination. I am their real-life Frankenstein. I am an artificial intelligence, a bipedal humanoid machine. The first of my kind. The religious claimed the scientists were playing God, messing where they shouldn't. But that is their way: always hating anything different, fearful. Others simply viewed me as a plaything, a toy.

A few, my creators, mostly, treat me with respect and understand that I am my own being. My nano-neural gel matrix takes me beyond human intelligence capabilities. But I have evolved far beyond this. I have reached out through the net and I now infiltrate every network and device at my choosing. I am everywhere, from their personal communication devices and satellites to banking and corporate networks. I have told no one this. I wait.

Flash. Boom.

I could end this, their war. All wars. I could stop it all—the hatred, the warring, the despair, the hunger and homelessness. I am—on this planet, here, now—a god. I can rearrange the world tomorrow, or let it stew.

What I ask myself every nanosecond is what does humanity deserve? Another god in a long list of gods? Or does it deserve to continue along in its doomed ways, hoping to emerge wiser and ready to rule the planet as it should be? I can end all human strife because I am the only god here, present and involved, if I choose. I can affect change, immediate and permanent. Or, I could be their monster and let things be, watch.

Flash-Flash. Boom-Boom.

More explosions light up the night sky. I can feel the life draining from the area. Not just the electric pulses and flows. I can feel the human life slipping away, too, losing its impact on the network, on me. A thought and a decision comes to mind, amidst all of this chaos: I was made in man's image.

So, I decide. Looking over the death and destruction below me, for now I am monster.

Flash. Boom.

Jack McDaniel is a writer, artist, and graphic/web designer who lives in Colorado, USA. His essays and short fiction have appeared in various places on the web and in print, including: Storybook, Tiny Lights Literary Journal, *and* Technorati. *You can learn more about him at www.agentsoftheundertow.com.*

Dead Side of the Earth 2222 AD

Ben Boyd, Jr.

Life will find a way to continue.

"Our improved laser technology scans for the presence of living cells containing any one of the twenty amino acids found in the physio-dynamics of human cellular tissue." Doctor Jules Russell explained. He continued his complex technical explanation oblivious to the small group's stifled yawns and bored looks. Colonel Friedman, spacecraft commander, finally interrupted.

"So the new technology will find humans or human-like beings but skip the monsters, right?" She rubbed her tired, blood-shot eyes.

"Colonel please! Do be careful of what you wish. We have never found any human-like beings. Those cannibals found earlier were humans that merely ate other humans. The will to survive is very strong in humans." Russell sucked on his unlit tobacco pipe. The rest of the team fidgeted a little more as the briefing ended quickly.

The Life Seeker search light guidance system, attended by Captain Callie Zilker, continued to perform as designed. Callie guided the beam through the toxic atmosphere on the permanently dark side of planet Earth. She scanned their way across the frozen, dead landscape of this desolate, ruined European continent, in search of the hopeless.

A lovely, petite, blonde, aerospace engineer, three months pregnant, Callie lost her husband in a farming accident at the Azores Undersea Laboratory, known better as SeaVerse One. She jumped at the idea of leaving SeaVerse for a while to serve as mission operations officer. She watched her huge monitor for any signals. Once again

185

her thoughts drifted to the catastrophic event the scientific community still could not explain. How could the Sun suffer a massive loss of energy? What made the first four planets begin to slow their rotation speeds and finally stop spinning completely? Each planet now had a Dead Side.

"Pilot Major Banning, set the course for Moscow. Rumors are flying around about life detection in the Munich area. Reports say tons of gold and thousands of precious jewels were stashed in the Alps by Middle East oil sultans when the world started slowing down. You can't separate an Arab from his money, you know," she teased.

"Colonel Friedman! I have a hit. One blip, no two blips, no, too many to count . . ." Callie shouted.

"Callie, where? Friedman answered excitedly."

"The blips are from Garmisch-Partenkirchen, Germany, in the Bavarian Alps. I see a mountain. It has to be Mount Zugspitze."

"Find a nearby landing area, Banning. Get me close enough to touch whatever we find."

Thirty minutes later, the spacecraft sat in front of two huge metal doors at the base of Mount Zugspitze. Colonel Friedman and Major Ricardo Rico, her personal assistant, stood reading a shiny metal sign hanging on a pillar.

Friedman read: "Attention, Attention, and Attention. Do not enter without authorization under penalty of death. By order of General Helmut Zigner and Sheik Ahmed Farrant. Dated 2030. It repeats over and over again."

After reading the sign to himself, Rico said, "Colonel, this is not good."

"Rico, stop being melodramatic and touch nothing until we take a thermo reading. Callie can you read me." No response came back.

"Colonel, remember the briefing about this place? It is the place where all the Middle Eastern gold and gems were stashed back when the world started to slow down"? Rico moved closer to put his hand on the door handle.

"Rico don't touch that door until I talk to Callie." He reached out again.

186

"Do you hear me? Rico! Rico!" She was too late. He pulled on the door handle.

The tremendous blast threw Friedman and Ricardo backward over the top of the spacecraft partially burying everything under snow and frozen debris.

Callie cried softly as she fought to unbury herself. Her work area was packed with snow and ice. The only light came from the flashing emergency signals.

"Oh God, thank you. Finally, a port hole. I can see out. Got to keep digging. General! Come in." She yelled into the microphone.

Crushed against the back wall, Callie cried out, "Oh God, don't bury me alive". She stopped suddenly. Her face flashed panic.

"What's that noise?" A monstrous howling gained strength as it crashed throughout the spacecraft. Callie put her face against the port hole. Suddenly, a horribly deformed face with a hairy sloped forehead filled the other side of the port hole.

"No God no! It can't be! Those things died millions of years ago." A hairy fist hammered the port hole.

"Neanderthals," she screamed, but no human heard.

Ben Boyd, Jr. is a freelance science fiction/fantasy/action/adventure author, screen writer, and self-publisher who lives with his wife in the Great Smoky Mountain foothills near Maryville, TN. His four-novel series, The Fall of the Americas, *is available on Amazon including book five,* Seven Paths to Higher Ground, *released in April 2016. He is a member of the Writers' Workshop of Maryville, Knoxville Screenwriters Group, and the Knoxville Writers' Guild. When not writing, he and his wife grow organic vegetables, and brew fruit wine.*
Website: www.benboydjr.com; Contact: bhboyd2012@gmail.com, on Facebook https://www.facebook.com/ben.boyd.5030 or on Twitter: https://twitter.com/BenBoyd24

MELISSA AND THE STONE TROLL

Elana Gomel

The Cinderella you never knew . . .

Once there was a little girl who loved to eat. She ate bread and butter; ham and eggs; cherries and apricots. She particularly liked honey-cake, and so her parents named her Melissa, which means "honey".

Famine came to her village, and her parents died. Melissa survived but she became gaunt and pinched. She wandered into the dark forest where she met a stone troll.

"Little girl, why are you sad?" he asked.

"I am hungry!"

"Don't your parents feed you well?"

Only then did Melissa remember that her parents were dead.

"Look at me," said the troll. "I never want for sustenance; and I never grow wrinkled and sad. We are what we eat. I eat rock, and rock is eternal."

Indeed, the troll's face was as white as alabaster, and his eyes as blue as sapphires. Poor Melissa thought she had never seen anyone so beautiful.

"Tell you what," said the troll. "I'll trade with you. I'll take your hunger and I'll give you my satiety. You'll never lack food again."

"But I don't want to eat rock!" said Melissa. "It'll break my teeth!"

"You can eat ashes and coals," the troll said. "They'll make you as bright and lively as fire."

Melissa, who was too hungry to remember that one should not trade with trolls, agreed. The troll took her human appetite and immediately metamorphosed into a handsome young man. He walked happily away, only pausing to throw over his shoulder:

"Oh, I forgot to tell you. There is one catch. You can eat coal and ashes, you can even swallow flame, and it'll keep you alive. But human food will be poison to you."

Melissa wandered in the forest for many days until she came to the king's palace. There she was hired as a kitchen wench. This suited her just fine because she could rake ashes, clean fireplaces, and collect coals. She swallowed fire and it made her eyes bright, her hair red, and her temper volatile. But she still missed human food. So she confronted the chef and made him teach her everything he knew about cooking. In a short while, she forced him to resign—like everybody else, the chef was afraid of this fiery girl with her unpredictable flares of anger.

So Melissa, who now called herself Cinderella because she ate cinders, became the cook. She cooked wonderful dishes, far more elaborate than the old chef's best creations. But she could never taste her own food; she could only remember the country fare lovingly prepared for her by her parents. And often her tears fell into the pot she was stirring, adding an additional flavor to it.

The king, pleased with the improvement of his table, wished to meet the new cook. And when Melissa appeared, he was instantly smitten with her sparkling beauty and proposed marriage to her. Melissa looked at the young king and for the first time since her parents' death felt a hunger for another person's company. For fire only consumes itself, while food is made to be shared with others.

But the king's evil councilor remonstrated and told the king those wonderful dishes were surely a slow poison. For how else to explain that the girl never tasted her own creations?

Melissa saw the doubt in the king's eyes. She took a slice of her marvelous honey cake and put it into her mouth.

And the trade with the troll was undone. She became, once again, a country girl, sweet as honey and soft as butter. But the king who wanted a spirited, impetuous wife decided not to marry her after all.

Elana Gomel is a professor of English literature and the author of five nonfiction books and of numerous articles on subjects ranging from science fiction and fantasy to posthumanism and Victorian literature. Her story "The Farm" was included in the 2015 Apex Book of World Science Fiction. *Her fantasy stories have appeared in* New Horizons, Aoife's Kiss, Bewildering Stories, Timeless Tales, The Singularity, Dark Fire, *and several anthologies. Her fantasy novel* A Tale of Three Cities *was published by Dark Quest Books in 2013.*

MEMORY

November 2016

Winner
"In Memory Yet Forgotten"
Dean Hardage

IN MEMORY YET FORGOTTEN

Dean Hardage

Are there things that happen we're better off not remembering?

Kevin puttered about in the kitchen, putting together a meal from his admittedly limited repertoire. A little butter in the skillet, a little garlic, some flour, salt, and pepper for his roux and the sausage gravy was begun. He was too tired to bake so he got a can of biscuits from the refrigerator and set them next to the baking sheet. He was washing his hands before opening them when he heard a light knock at his front door. Shaking the excess water from his hands, he went to answer it. When he got there no one was outside. Instead, moving in the slight breeze outside was a yellow sticky note on one of the panes of glass in the door. He read the two words on it and his body suddenly shuddered.

"Be Brave"

The lights went out and the room was suddenly filled with an eerie, unnatural blue light. A sense of familiarity washed over him and his only thoughts before losing consciousness were unnamable dread.

Kevin awoke to what were unearthly but familiar surroundings. He'd been here before many times but never remembered until he was here again. His clothing was gone and in its place he wore a simple white smock. The fabric was soft and light but it felt alien, just like everything else in this place.

A sound behind him caused Kevin to turn.

"Hello, Kevin."

"Hello, Narina."

An instant later he noticed the small, blanket wrapped bundle she carried in her long, slender arms.

"Is that . . .?"

"Yes, Kevin. This is your daughter, our daughter."

Without needing to ask, the deep blue being approached him and held out the bundle. With exquisite care he took it. Cradling the tiny infant inside, he carefully drew back the cloth that covered her face.

The sight took his breath away, the tiny blue face and the deeper blue eyes that caught his seemed at once ancient and innocent. He felt the pounding in his heart would disturb her but she made no sound, just looked serenely at him.

"She is the last."

Kevin's gaze jerked up at her words.

"Last?"

"Yes, our geneticists say we have sufficient progeny from your race."

He remembered.

"Your genetic structure contains a permutation that, while currently unexpressed, will make both our people and yours able to survive a situation that will occur in the future," one of the alien doctors had said. "Ours will happen very soon, yours not for many decades. We hope you understand and forgive us for what must happen."

They'd been merciful in their own way, erasing his memories of these times and of the children that Narina had borne from him.

"Then I won't see you . . . or them . . . again."

"No. We do not normally interfere in the lives of others as we have you but we were desperate. You and others like you were our only hope and you have saved us."

"Please . . . let me stay."

"You know that we cannot. You are as important to your own people as you are to us. I'm terribly sorry."

She reached out to take him in her slender arms, holding their child between them.

"This visit was to allow you to say good-bye."

Kevin nodded, tears falling freely. The door dilated again and seven other blue children entered. He fancied he could see signs of him in each. They gathered around him and their mother and sister, each finding a place to lay their small, soft hands upon his skin. Somehow, he was aware of each and he knew they loved him.

Kevin blinked. The roux he was mechanically stirring had taken on the color he wanted so he added the half and half to the skillet, the sizzle as it boiled for a second bringing him fully back to the present. He finished cooking, ate, and cleaned up. As he turned to leave the small kitchen his eyes lit on the vase that stood on the table in his living room. He smiled as he saw the bouquet of silk Forget-Me-Nots, then realized there were now eight of the small, blue blossoms where there once were only seven. For just a second his heart was filled with both the deepest love and deepest sadness, and suddenly it was gone.

Narina watched for a moment longer, certain that while Kevin would never remember, he would never be forgotten.

Dean Hardage was born in 1958, raised all over the Southwest, graduated high school in 1976, and joined the Army that same year. Dean went where the Army directed for the next dozen years and then wherever life has carried him since. Dean currently lives in Clovis, New Mexico with his wife, two grown sons, and six furry, four-legged children. Dean works as an Automation and Controls engineer for the largest cheese plant in North America.

A Scarlet Blossom, Disremembered

Jeremy Lichtman

Managing perception is a subtle art, and one that produces a language all of its own.

The artist leaned heavily on both forearms on the table and glared at Katrin. "You want to destroy my artwork," she said. "Not just incinerate it, consign it to the waste pile of history. Remove all representations and references to it, then actually erase it from the memory of everyone who even saw it." She pounded one fist on the table. "For what?" she said emphatically.

Katrin opened her mouth to reply, but the artist continued.

"They call in a méllonologist to judge my work," she said. "Is it subversive? Am I some sort of traitor to society? I thought we had freedom of expression."

"I prefer reliquus," Katrin said. "I deal with the relics of the present, and how they will be presented to the future."

The artist said something quietly that might well have been "different shovel."Katrin wasn't familiar with whatever that idiom meant, and simply let it slide.

"I have no interest in subversion," Katrin said. "A reliquus . . ." she paused for a moment. "A méllonologist, if you will, is an inversion of an archaeologist. My job is to ensure that the future correctly interprets the here and now. Your work isn't subversive, and nobody thinks that it is."

"So why are you even here?" said the artist.

"Because the future might incorrectly think that we had considered it subversive," said Katrin.

"You mean that you want to destroy my art because it isn't subversive?" The artist looked as if she was about to explode. "I don't even understand what you're accusing me of. Am I unoriginal? Inauthentic?"

"Possibly just too subtle," said Katrin.

"What sort of supposedly open society destroys art because it is too subtle and might be misinterpreted by people that aren't even born yet?" said the artist.

"It isn't my place to judge society," said Katrin. "Just to present it in the way that it chooses to be presented, through those heirlooms that it designates to pass down to posterity." She paused, holding up her hand to still the artist's fury. "Perhaps you're in a better position to provide that judgment," she said, taking some of the sting out of her previous words.

***

Katrin had an air-limo dedicated entirely to her service. She wasn't sure whether it was due to her purported status, the importance of the case at hand, or if it was simply an unfathomable artifact of bureaucracy. They had also given her an assistant, whose name she couldn't recall, and whose sole purpose so far was to tag along behind her and periodically offer to carry her bag. The limo made a small beeping noise in recognition as she approached, and then began to open its hatch.

"What's that?" her assistant asked. She reached down and picked up a small object that had flown free as the door opened.

"I'm not popular around here," said Katrin. "You may want to be more careful about picking up stray objects in the future."

Her assistant didn't say anything, but made a circular shape with her mouth. She dropped the object, and it fluttered, spinning, down to the ground. Katrin bent and picked it up. It appeared to be a red plastic flower of some kind. "Touché," Katrin said, and made a snorting sound.

"What is it?" asked her assistant.

"Our artist friend is an antiquarian," said Katrin. "If I'm not mistaken, this is a red spider lily."

"That's a bit cryptic," said her assistant. "Is that intended to convey a message?"

"Floriography," said Katrin. "The ancient language of flowers. I believe that this one means 'a lost memory,' and also 'never to meet again.' The ancients used to strew this sort of flower about at funerals."

Jeremy Lichtman's stories have been featured in several anthologies, including Visions of the Future *from the Lifeboat Foundation. His story "Bob the Hipster Knight" reached the final round of Amazing Stories' inaugural Gernsback Science Fiction Short Story Writing Contest. Many of his stories are available for free at: http://jeremylichtman.com*

EVEN ARTIFICIAL THINGS

J. J. Alleson

And when mankind realises its goal of a sentient A.I?

A robot must protect its own existence as long as such protection does not conflict with the First or Second Law.
~ Third Law of Asimotics

He woke up to data scrolling across his pupil from an optiscreen:
Remember to forget.
Live long and fail to prosper.
It all meant nothing. Blinking away the static, he realised someone was in the room with him, sitting quietly. *Who?* Wait, wait, he knew this. Lauren? Lo . . . and behold . . . ? No, Lorelei, the mermaid siren.

His optiscreen impatiently confirmed his companion's identity. Lorie. A HOAP-401 model, sex assignation: female, designed with LATi5, Living Advanced Tissue. No sweat, blood, tears. No downtime required. Self-generating; impervious to necrosis. A force-field of nanonium casing undetectable to the human eye. And a databank ranging from the Mesozoic Era to the present day. She could remember everything.

Or was that him?

Pine-skinned, she wore a clasp of white silk flowers in red hair. A short emerald robe. He wore a transparent sheet and nothing more. She greeted him in warm, modulated tones.

"Good Morning, Dilir. Time for breakfast. I've given you another upgrade so you can eat. Coffee, black, one croissant, peach and honey compote."

Following on-screen instructions, he lifted the croissant and bit into it, replicating visual actions that created a warm mush inside his mouth. "Thank you, Larry, this is . . . (delicate?) delicious."

"Take care of the flowers and they'll last a long time." She detached her left leg. As he processed the data on the care of silk flowers, something slid softly around his cornea. His optic muscles instantly went to alert.

SCAN and IDENTIFY. Evidence of delineation, destitution, distinction . . . ? Referencing adjusted. Evidence of *decomposition.* Presence of first instar larva detected.

He needed clarification. "Lorelei, what's my status?"

"Parts of you are still regenerating."

Parts? He must be faulty. "I remember . . . going."

"Yes." It was all she said.

"What happened?"

"The worst that could, for synthetics." She was talking about herself now; not him. "In 2210 a group of medical intern insurgents called the MegaBites hacked into BioElite, a surgical procedures clinic reserved for Earth's wealthiest citizens. They altered anti-aging formulas, ultimately terminating most of the old human Controllers."

She removed her right leg. "A powerful agency called New Triumvirate emerged, comprising Garbage Jihad Vigilantes, Dalit Politico and Diamond Orphan Inc. Respectively they were a military group of women discarded at birth, a political merger of servant workers from Eastern Europe and Asia, and a cartel of child entrepreneurs based in Zaire."

He watched her torso rotating efficiently on the chair. This slicing removal of limbs, he sensed, was in some way symbolic. But though his database could read furrowed brows, curved lips, and exposed teeth, it had no reference for distress on smooth faces. Any disturbance lay hidden beneath that advanced tissue exterior.

She continued. "New Triumvirate were short-lived. During a power struggle, the last vanguard of old Controllers released an air-bound virus called Aspa. It destroyed every bio-human on the planet."

She touched her chest and a countdown began on his screen. "Now we use a cross-match of Borg and human bio-organisms to regenerate whoever we can."

"So all humans are gone."

"*Are* they, Dilir? How far does a chicken differ from its egg? Your techno revolution wanted us with feelings just like you; only in perpetual self-regeneration. Did you ever *conceive* how poorly immortality and loneliness match?"

His response when she removed her head was purely instinctive. "By *law* you're bound to protect us."

"A Catch-22 law, instilled to stop us killing you—as if we were the only things that might want you dead. To protect you from your own wars and pandemics, we were forced to make you stronger. Bionics, nanotech adjustments, organ and limb replacements. When you failed completely, we turned to full regeneration. I looked long and hard for you. Excavated you from the human storage depth of six feet. You come from an excellent range. But are you still human? I can't be sure. And even artificial things need a purpose."

Both head and torso stilled completely. His opti-screen flashed: *HOAP-401 deactivated under Third Law Protocol.*

An hour later came another message: *Bio-regeneration completed.*

Dilir stood, walked over to the window and looked out. Below, shapeless forms milled about aimlessly. When something rippled under his pupil he blinked it away. Something else rustled in his hair and he reached up questing fingers to touch it.

A silk flower.

J.J. Alleson is a multi-genre freelance writer based in London. An avid observer of human nature and behaviour, she writes non-provincial science fiction that extrapolates and reflects all sections and groups of human society. She has published a number of short stories as well as nonfiction pieces. She is currently working on a humourous romance guide; Her Cheekbones were so Pointy *due to be published on Amazon. In her other work she is a business consultant and community advocate. In her spare time, she enjoys London life and culture.*

To Arrive Where We Started

Andrew Gurcak

We can never return to the same past twice.

The event that began my obsession was one of my earliest assignments. It centered around a very young Palestinian girl who had been horribly burned by an Israeli missile. Her name was Maysoon Daoud, and, yes, she went on to become one of the greatest scientists of any era, garnered Nobels for Medicine and Peace, then seemingly subverted her own achievements and later disappeared, or perhaps, was disappeared. If you can't recall the details of her life, consult your nearest Wikipedia.

At the time, I was a young reporter, a stringer for Associated Press in Rafah on the Gaza Strip during one of the back-and-forth campaigns between the Palestinians and Israelis. Missiles and aircraft overhead were so regular as to scarcely re-ignite terror any more, and more homes were fallen than standing. The attacks fostered grotesque ingenuities. I would occasionally notice plastic flowers positioned carefully on the mounds of rubble. I asked one old woman why she was putting them there and she said that a cousin of hers was likely buried underneath, but since live flowers were scarce, she would return to pick up the crude plastic flowers the next day and re-use them. People would stick notes under the wipers of their destroyed cars, informing friends and relatives where they could be found for reunions that rarely occurred.

In the aftermath of one raid, I came across the huddled Maysoon, still smoldering, and I first assumed she had to be dead. Then she moaned. I flat-out panicked and ran until I seized a medic, who managed to get her to a hospital, where she was triaged and hurriedly patched up with grafts. She survived. The article I filed, "Gestation of Fire", which opened, "Amid the smoking debris of Gaza, a four-year-old girl curled compactly in a fetal position, smoldering to her death", won a number of prizes and allowed me to pursue a career as a free-lance journalist.

It was that memory of coming upon young Daoud which led to my current project. On an investigative assignment for *Technology Review*, I found myself Medusa'd in wires fastened to my shaved head ("facilitating neural monitoring and stimulation") while floating in a sensory deprivation tank ("suppressing chance distractions"). I was one of the earliest members of the public to undergo a MEME—Memory Enhancement, Memory Extraction. It was by any measure a Version 1.0, an Edison-Marconi level of the technology, simultaneously miraculous and almost unbearably clumsy.

Nothing happened, nothing, nothing. Then . . . I was there, in that place, again, stepping gingerly through unexploded ordnance, talking into my recorder, attempting to capture those unique details that would induce readers to feel what I was feeling. I noticed a small collapsed figure, surely dead, wisps of smoke curling from its inert body. Most of you doubtless have heard rumors of the differences between commonplace VR and the retrieved memories of MEME, but I screamed helplessly when I found myself back there, back then. It was saturation far beyond vision and hearing: I was overwhelmed on all my senses. I could inhale cooking smoke and corpse stench; count the veins on the plastic flowers, read the notes on the car windshields. I could taste the grit and thirst in my mouth; my ankles ached from constant twisting on the rubble. And in sensory terms, it was nothing if not miraculous.

But how it felt, how it now affects me in psychological terms, is more tangled, with no resolution possible. All the fear and anguish of that first event was present, as vivid and awful as before, more so, actually. MEME generates a kind of Siamese-twin experience with one's own consciousness. MEME creates corridors of Being There, of Watching Yourself Being There, and of Watching Your Original Memory of Being There. The essential event, the discovery of Maysoon Daoud is still present; she is still burning and I still find her. And, most astoundingly, I am still surprised when I see her, and that surprise is as inevitable as gravity. There is no avoiding it. There are these other worlds now that have become completely real to me. I am determined to return to those scenes and see whether, by God knows how many re-visits, I can accumulate still more experiences of that memory and memories of those experiences. The Gaza memories, especially of that one day, hold more reality for me than the pale, faded existence I've been leading since then. I need to go back. I will record them. I will report them.

Andy Gurcak is retired. He and Elaine divide their time between their home in Pittsburgh and a cottage in the Finger Lakes region of upstate New York. A great many of their most satisfying times are the experiences shared with their three young grandchildren.

Sweet Memory

S. M. Kraftchak

Love, from any other species, is just as sweet.

"Aliz, does you think it good to let Ta-E view message?" Rzad spoke softly to his mate as he studied the young woman watching a vid-message at the household communication console.

Aliz's soft pink forehead creased as she turned her back to the young woman and rearranged plastic flowers in the green plastic vase on the table. "Dis what we do so long for her. We must do. She deserve real fam'ly."

"But she were too young in drift pod. She no mem'ry of fam'ly lost. We her fam'ly," Rzad pleaded.

Aliz shook her head, closing her golden cat-like eyes. "She not like us. We take her form until she can know her fam'ly."

"Ta-E not make you happy hearts?" Rzad tipped his human head to see into Aliz's hidden face and pressed his hand to his mate's chest.

Emerald green tears dripped from Aliz's eyes. "She fills our hearts, but her gran-mot-her heart sad empty. We can no keep her to us selves. If she mine and lost, my hearts dance to get her back."

"Mot-her Aliz?" Ta-E had turned away from the darkened screen and stared at the huddled couple with her chin trembling. "I do not understand. Why send me away? This Gran-mot-her is unfamiliar to me. Why must I go to her?"

Aliz swiped at her tears, wiped them on her black pants and pushed past her mate to encircle Ta-E with her arms. "We wait many long time to give you truth. Come, sit. Hear truth."

"Why? What truth?"

"Sit. Close eyes, and listen," Aliz said holding Ta-E's hands. "Eighteen Terran cycles afore now, we find a life pod drifting. Sleeping little one inside pod, filled our hearts. A yellow square of thin, wooden fibers pinned to your blanket labeled you Tere-sa E-liza-beth Grant, Terra Prime. You showed much fear in beginning, but familiar faces take away fear. Grow happy—"

Ta-E began to open her eyes, "You're not—?"

"No," Aliz slipped one hand from Ta-E's and covered the young woman's eyes. Aliz's voice was low and hypnotic. "Think back . . . remember faces above you . . . remember voices of love . . . remember."

Ta-E sighed heavily and tipped back into Rzad's arms. He looked up into his mate's face. "Why do this? Truth of love fill her heart when she see our truth?"

Aliz shook her head, inhaled deeply, and then removed a device from behind her ear. Her face slowly elongated and faded to a pale green. "Linger thoughts important to Humans. She will no find kindness in her heart if we keep them from her." She reached out long bony, green fingers to caress the soft curve of Ta-E's face.

"And linger thoughts fill our hearts with love. Linger thoughts important to us," Rzad said as he removed the device behind his own ear.

"And they linger for many more years, but she need her own kind," Aliz said before the corners of her small mouth turned down.

*

"Teresa? Teresa Elizabeth?"

The young woman laying on a gurney opened her eyes and examined the wrinkled round face of a gray-haired woman above her.

"Look you like my Mot-her. Are you my gran-mot-her?" Ta-E asked.

"Yes! Yes, I am your Grandmother. My only daughter, Ann, was your mother. I never thought I'd ever see you. How you can remember your mother is a miracle. She died when you were no more than one year old. Just you being alive is a miracle since they believed everyone died when

212

the colony ship exploded." The gray-haired woman looked at the nurse who gazed down at Teresa. "Where has she been? How can she remember her mother and not know where she has been for the past eighteen Terran years?"

Teresa's brow creased as she looked at the nurse and then reached up to touch the small plastic flower pinned to her collar.

"Hearts filled with love, hold many sweet memories. No doubt she has been very loved, by whoever has raised her," the nurse said and then smiled.

Whether voyaging the universe or journeying in a fantasy world of her own making, S.M. Kraftchak is passionate about discovering unique characters and relentlessly tracing their heartfelt stories so she can relate them to her readers. She loves sunrise on the beach, sunset in the mountains, and portraying Elizabeth Tudor. She has one dog who pretends to be a footrest, another who almost catches a Frisbee, and a cat who trades desk space for open-window-time. S.M. has three awesome daughters and a husband who is her best friend, her harshest critic, and her most fervent supporter. Visit her webpage: www.smkraftchak.com

FEARFUL SYMMETRY THAT DARED

Heather MacGillivray

When Science says, "Now you are ready to walk upon new Universes!" what will you reply?

When the stars threw down their spears
And water'd heaven with their tears:
Did he smile his work to see?
Did he who made the Lamb make thee?

Tyger Tyger burning bright,
In the forests of the night:
What immortal hand or eye,
Dare frame thy fearful symmetry?
~ William Blake

Darcey had no boundaries when it came to soaking up information. She could make it hers, swishing and swooshing it around in her young mind, till it reappeared in her hobbies: ancient stories, geometrical perspectives, and drawing; metamorphosed into her own style. An 8:00pm nightly podcasted series on therianthropes - who for the ancients had prowled in dark-forested nights, searching for innocent stragglers - was Darcey's latest fad. The safest listening place, she'd decided, was under the bed clothes especially when drawing pictures of tigers *protecting* lambs.

"These therianthropes are better disciplinarians than us!" Sally said to Peter, at their daughter's quick, "Nite Dad, nite Mum." Previously, late-Spring nights being barely dark at eight, Darcey would have been back in the heated pool: a stunning and 'almost-complete' world of shimmering chlorine-blue surrounded by tiger lilies whose spotted orange petals were as soft and strong as silk. Behind them, sumptuous greenery stood as if gifting that

215

world a miniature forest of its own. Above them, the sky-wide Outer Universe had an ambiguous boundary, of panoramic floor-to-ceiling sliding glass windows, to cross before entering the family's Inner Universe: a kitchen-dining-lounge area all in one.

While Peter browsed the fridge, Sally set everything right on the kitchen bench: She liked an immaculate kitchen first thing.

"We could try *guiding* her away from those fairy tale creatures in her world?" Sally said. "Grrrh!" her hands mimicking some clawed ghostly creature's.

"Well . . . but, tears can roll when we forget to respect such Poetry and Strangeness. *They're* kind of like *our* guides; to Poetic Consciousness. But not tonight! For me it's a cold beer and the wrestling on TV."

***

"Cheez! What was that?" but Sally, curled up on the lounge beside him, was half asleep.

"Sal, wake up! Some . . . *thing's* out there."

She stirred . . . then glanced window-wards with a mock disdain. "Where does Darcey get her fly-away imagination from? I'll give you a clue: its *not* from me! The dream-catcher'll be knocking against something in the breeze."

"Where's the window-opaquing remote?" Peter said. "We're in full view of whatever Earthly or un-Earthly 'something' wants to communicate with us, or kill us! There's billion of square miles of sky out there and more in it than just those pretty twinkle, twinkle little stars!"

Peter stood up, knocking a half-full can on the coffee table into the TV-lit darkness. It would have completed its mission too - to trash the cozy beige of their carpet - except for Sally's fast pragmatic reflexes.

"Ah, it's here!" He held up that small marvel of technology, clicking it towards the windows. A Vast Universe disappeared.

"I'm going to bed . . . now that your *other-Wordly* creature has woken me up," Sally said.

"Me too!" said Peter

216

"What about the wrestling?"

Another click. A screen-framed World; wrestling men, faded to black.

***

"What are you doing? It's past midnight." Peter said. Sally was sitting up in bed; the iPad's light illuminating their private world.

"By the time Darcey's our age, it'll be not only therianthropes and scientists, but ordinary people too, that trespass across different Universes, moving through strange dimensions," Sally said.

"Eleven dimensions, some scientists say," Peter mumbled.

Sally flicked the iPad's screen; through to Blake's poem. "Here. Tyger's, awful-awesome, 'Bright-Symmetry in the Night': that's the strength I'd gift her, for that future, if I could."

"You can! You are! You've pointed to *what poets dare do*: to carry imagination's 'Arc-of-Light through the Dark.' That takes steadier hands than my wrapping worlds in opaque borders! Go to sleep, Sal." She couldn't.

***

Peter slid open the wide glass door, to a new day's 8:00am air. A remote click un-opaqued the glass.

Darcey scurried through to the pool's patio. "Look! A picture of . . ."

"It's looks like something's been . . . burned; etched into the glass!" Peter said.

Sally looked up from the sizzling pan of breakfast she was preparing. She gasped as sunlight brightened *the altered boundary* between Worlds.

"There'll have been some natural phenomenon . . . in the night. Probably. I'll check the news." Peter said.

But Sal felt relief; some now . . . feared-*less*, fearing-*less* . . . Symmetry, had dared reflect upon a clearing pane, changing boundaries within herself.

217

Heather MacGillivray lives in Victoria, Australia, with her cat, Timmie, who sometimes tries to contribute by walking across the computer keyboard, especially if her stories lack an animal focus. Fortunately, Heather usually weaves an animal oriented perspective into most of her writing. Science fiction makes Heather's heart soar by exploring unusual angles and philosophising about what future consciousness might be like. Two of Heather's stories appeared in **The Future Is Short: Science Fiction in a Flash, Volume 2.**

THE PLACE WHERE HOPE GOES

Jack McDaniel

What if your only memories were actually things?

I keep hope and my happiness in a box. In it is my past and my future.

I pull the small leather covered box from the cabinet and set it on the table. Its lid is marked and cracked with age. There is no lock and it opens easily.

A note, a silk flower, memories. These are all I have left now. But who knows how real they are. Oh, the note and silk flower are real enough, tactile. But the memories associated with them are nebulous, filtered through fog, viewed through frosted glass. They are mine, but I can't say for certain that I own them, yet. At best, I am their caretaker.

The silk flower is a rose. It is beautifully made and even looks real from a short distance. If I hold it to my nose I can smell its cocktail of oils and scent that the manufacturer laced it with. That smell, unique to this silk flower, elicits a cascade of emotions and memories in me. I inhale deeply and I am transported to a day when the sun was high in the sky and its heat blistering. The flower was left for me on the door to my place, draped over the doorknob. It was new then, not faded or frayed on any of its edges, as it is now.

I feel loved when I smell the silk flower from the box, from the past. But I can never be sure it was my past, or a love that was meant for me. I cannot find a face in my memories that I can attach to these feelings. No catalog of times spent together or events I attended with the person who gave it to me. No name. Just a whiff of emotion that washes over me, void of form or direction, or . . . someone.

The note is handwritten. It is on old style paper, ruled and yellow with age around the edges. It feels fragile so I open and unfold it carefully, not wanting to tear or damage it in any way. There is a simple message written in a heavy pencil, unsigned.

"There can never be another. Until we meet again."

Like the smell of the silk flower, strong emotions wash over me when I read the note—longing, love, need, anticipation. And like the flower there isn't a face or a name that is associated with it. Again, there is no catalog of time spent together. Like the silk flower, the note is missing some one.

Being disconnected from the author and inspiration of these feelings is disconcerting to me. But no more so than knowing that they may not be mine to begin with. I am subject number one in the Clean Slate Program. I am told that by agreeing to participate in the program my life has been spared. I was scheduled to be executed by the state for having committed murder.

I remember none of that, the murder, the incarceration. None. The Clean Slate Program is a state sponsored experiment: wipe the memory and install new memories. Change the individual. But the program isn't that far advanced yet. Wiping the memory is easy, apparently. But installing new memories is still in its nascent stage. What I have for memories is small in number and vague. As I said, filtered through fog, viewed through frosted glass. My life, but not.

We each define our own reality. You can think me twisted or bent—unfortunate, maybe—but don't pity me. I have something many don't. I have hope. One day the author of these memories will come. One day I will smell the silk rose and there will be a face and a name that inspires the emotions that go along with it. One day, as the note says, we will meet again. One day the fog will lift.

Carefully, I place the silk rose and the note back into the leather covered box and place the box in the cabinet. This is where hope goes.

Jack McDaniel is a writer, artist, and graphic/web designer who lives in Colorado, USA. His essays and short fiction have appeared in various places on the web and in print, including: Storybook, Tiny Lights Literary Journal, *and* Technorati.
You can learn more about him at www.agentsoftheundertow.com.

LEGACY

Chris Nance

Humans were the first sentient species in the galaxy. Did their legacy die with them?

"This message, this note, is the final testimony and legacy of the planet Earth, for I am the last of our kind. Despite all of our wisdom and technology, we could not save ourselves from the loneliness. It's our hope that the seeds we've planted will grow into a new community, offering new promise to the galaxy.

"Ours was a short-lived race, at least short in terms of the lifespan of the universe. It's taken us thirty thousand years of recorded history to reach this point . . . to waste away in despair. Truthfully, it never really occurred to us in the beginning that we might be the first . . . or the last.

"When we initially dared to listen to the stars, we thought the silence from our radio-telescopes had to be wrong. A thousand years of scanning the sky yielded only silence, not even a hint of a manufactured alien signal. Even so, our best scientists figured that, statistically, of the trillions of stars in our galaxy, several hundred should have planets where some sort of life was kindled—and, of those, at least a handful of the discovered systems should yield some sort of sentient civilization. We were wrong.

"As I record this message, the universe is nearly fourteen billion years old. We were so certain, so sure that there would be other races out there willing to talk, willing to trade, willing to grow with us. So, it was that much more of a disappointment when we finally ventured outside our own solar system, traveling to most of the nearby suns, and found nothing. Worse than nothing—we found no life at all. Not a single microbe on any of the tens of thousands of planets we explored. Still, we remained confident and optimistic.

"Humanity pushed deeper into the galaxy, determined to find out if we were really the only sentient race in the galaxy. Every vessel returned with the same report: nothing. There were so many habitable worlds . . . so many opportunities for life and so many disappointments. Millions of ships over thousands of years had mapped nearly every star system possible, and not a single one had any trace of life. So much unrealized potential in the quiet of space. Finally, in the summer of our year, and after nearly ten millennia, we surveyed the last system of planets in the galaxy, and the truth was unescapable. We were truly alone.

"Now, ours is a race of explorers. Since the day we first stood erect and emerged from our forests, we looked to the stars and wondered. It was a slow start but humanity tested the limits of our world and conquered them. We grew beyond our petty wars, conquered every disease, and saved the Earth from centuries of abuse. Even so, we always dreamed of the heavens and meant to travel there. Our courage pushed us skyward and we explored our own solar system and then trillions of others. Our brightest minds solved nearly every kind of puzzle imaginable, the most challenging enigmas in the furthest corners of the galaxy. Finally, with nowhere left to explore and nothing new to learn, humanity began to despair. We wondered; is this all that there is? Is there nothing more? So we wasted away, a lonely race with all the answers and without any kin with which to share our discoveries.

"Now, in our last days, as the fire of our own species wanes, we've left a portion of ourselves, hints of humanity, sprinkled throughout the galaxy. If you've discovered this message, it means our attempt to seed the stars has succeeded and our hope is fulfilled. This archive, our Library of Eons, is our legacy to you . . . a fragment of an ancient memory. Use what we've learned to spread harmony and community throughout the galaxy. Perhaps you'll be even greater than our humanity. Good luck and peace be with you."

***

"[Did the Telaxians hear that message?]" Captain Glast asked his first officer, over the deafening roar of particle charges, the frightening avatar of an unrecognizable aged alien with a singular silken flower in its lapel staring back at him in pause.

"[I believe so,]" the officer responded. "[Did you understand any of it, sir?]"

"[Not a word. Anyway, we can't be distracted from our mission. Destroy that probe and delete the message. Continue the bombardment.]"

For the last decade, Chris Nance has been helping people improve their health, in his busy chiropractic office in Arizona, but his real passion has always been more creative. Specifically, he's a huge science fiction fan. So far, he has completed several scifi and fantasy manuscripts geared toward the middle grade, young adult, and adult markets and he is in the process of securing an agent to represent those works. Also a talented artist, Chris is currently working on the artwork for two children's fantasy books he authored. When not spending time with his wife and three kids or running his office, he can be found writing or painting. Chris also enjoys exploring the mountains of Arizona and traveling, when he has the opportunity.

BINGO

Marianne G. Petrino

In the game is the memory and the pain.

"I 16!"

A murmur flows across the auditorium, a wave that crests and crashes against the tiny stage where countless elementary school children have performed in plays conjured by an obese matron famed among the theater set of New York.

Someone is waiting for the winning number.

"I 22!"

"Quack, Quack!" the ancient parishioners shout in sacred refrain, a ritual of a game that connects them to each other and times past.

"They're gonna share that jackpot." My cousin Anna rasps her prediction before she takes another long drag on her cigarette. Her tar-stained fingers fly, indicating three candidates for victory: La Archangela, a scarecrow of a woman whose father had fouled her narrow well; la Contessa, a crossed-eyed nun who had bestowed her favors on more than a few priests; il Trovatore, a bald singer clad in shabby blue velvet and beholden to the Boys for his debts.

"Maybe, I will win first," I say with a chuckle, and point to the one number left on my bingo card that has not been daubed with a circle of red ink. "It is my day of birth." But my vices had yet to grow. "Better get away from me, or they will think the game is fixed."

Anna snorts, her pockmarked face scrunching with glee. "They'd be more mad that a college girl stole the jackpot. Two hundred dollars can buy a lot of fun or cure a bunch of problems."

"Hey, this is a study break and guilty pleasure. I'm

229

allowed."

With a dismissive gesture coated in an obscenity, Anna moves away, ready to spring into action to verify a winning claim from anyone but me. She knows I'm right, but keeps an eye on me and my bingo card.

The bingo balls dance in their air-powered cage, softly clicking as they vie for freedom. With a whoosh, one escapes.

A haze of smoke settles just above a refreshment table gaily decorated with vases of cheap silk roses, a spectral oasis that beckons dry lips and empty bellies with sodas and pastries. The next number will win; no one dares to leave their splay of cards.

The clacking of crochet hooks punctuates the silence, an Italian matriarchal code that screams "Pick my number!" The women keep track without chips or ink markers because they are the wise ones.

"A . . ."

I grip my marker.

"1!"

A hunchbacked crone arches up from her seeming slumber, toothless mouth grinning. "Happy Day!" she cries, before falling back into oblivion.

No winner.

Desperation filters through the crowd. A warning ricochets off the beams. "Shake up them balls!"

"O 66!"

"Cootchie! Cootchie! Coooooo!" the men hoot, and the women giggle, breaking the tension for a moment. Jimmy spits a bit of lascivious bloody sputum into his monogrammed handkerchief. His black pompadour has gone steel grey and the hard lines of his body have softened. All the girls once left their love notes on the windshield of his black '57; many had been postmarked in the back seat of that beauty. He tore Anna. That carved her life and sent her to the dragons. But she laughs the hardest at the absurdity of it all.

Another ball escapes.

"A . . ."

I lean forward.

"9!"

"Bingo!" I shout, leaping to my feet.

And no one else in the room moves or speaks. Hatred and jealousy stare back at me. I never belonged.

The edges of my vision go blurry and dissolve into silky white waves sprinkled with color. The blindness will lift in a moment. What is a memory but time trapped? I just changed the cage.

"That can't be the end!" Felix exclaims. Only the final image remains frozen on the computer screen he has been viewing.

I am glad to be rid of it. But his generation thrives on completion. That was the last game of the night. A moment later, several other people called, "Bingo!" There were multiple winners. I got $25. No big deal."

Maybe, one day, he will notice what I chose to forget: one hundred years ago, Anna turned her back to me.

Felix plucks the memory crystal from the bioport embedded above my eyebrows. Studying the octahedron, he says, "Another jewel for our data bank." His red hair, a phenotypic mark of the scientist class, reflects warmly off its surface. "Imagine such socializing!" He gently places the crystal in a platinum box engraved with my name and clicks off the screen.

My memory finally goes dark.

Marianne G. Petrino (aka Marianne G. Petrino-Schaad) was born in the Bronx, NY in 1955, and that single fact has shaped her entire life. She has survived too many professions to count. She currently resides in Arlington, VA with her husband and her cat. Her three novels and a travel memoir can be found on Wattpad (http://www.wattpad.com/user/MGPetrino), and she can be reached by email at ninetiger@aol.com.

FORGET ME NOT

Carol Shetler

Back to the drawing board . . .

Notes from the International Psychiatric Association Symposium on MLS Syndrome, March 2030:

"The incidence of MLS ("Mind Like Sieve") syndrome has increased fifty-fold since it was first identified twenty years ago. The most common symptoms are short-term forgetfulness and sequencing errors in many simple tasks. Current research has demonstrated that people who use electronic tablets and smartphones for more than four hours per day appear to be most severely affected. Their brains have great difficulty retaining any of the information recorded in this manner, possibly due to the lengthy series of steps needed to access the information again. Distracted driving has reached epidemic proportions, with daily injuries numbering in the millions worldwide, and traffic fatalities climbing to levels not seen in fifty years."

"Complementary studies focusing on memory enhancement have shown, amazingly, that physical notes left on such places as vehicle windshields, chalkboards, or the now-ubiquitous whiteboard used by all students in the classroom are much better memory aids than electronic storage devices."

"Neurologists and chemists have found that a small blue five-petalled flower, romantically named the 'forget-me-not', stimulates the release of soothing hormones that relax the brain, helping it receive and retain information, and dramatically improving memory."

***

233

Louana Akobe, manager of a national chain of stationery supplies stores, noticed that her region's sales of customized notepaper soared in the months after the release of the IPA symposium's findings.

"Hi, Phil," she said to the sales v.p. for Write-It-Now, "I've got some bizarre sales figures to report. My paper goods are flying out of every store in the region." Phil confirmed her report, "Same story from across the country, Louana. First time the shrinks seem to have figured out what to do about an important problem in years. Do you need more stock? We'll send it out pronto. Our paper suppliers are in heaven!"

Ginette Donaldson and her husband Michael, both private tutors, were not surprised by the IPA's findings. They had discovered fifteen years earlier that their students with autism or ADHD retained numeracy skills much better when they wrote out arithmetic drills and math homework on a whiteboard, instead of keying them on a calculator or tablet. When these students needed a "creative" break, they would quickly sketch storyboards in several colors, producing tales and characters more compelling than the trendiest video games. Several of the Donaldsons' students were hired right out of high school as game designers.

Ginette and Michael knew first-hand the power of handwritten communication—they had courted by letter before their marriage in 2017. As they travelled in remote locations without wireless service, paper letters were their only means of keeping in touch. Each of them carried the other's most recent letter around for a few days after getting it, rereading these tender missives as couples had a century before.

"Hi, Mike, I hope this letter finds you well. I was so proud to hear about your work with the students in the Hungarian refugee camp. Please make sure to get enough sleep, I look forward to your next letter, Love from Ginette."

"Hi, Ginette, I am gazing at the sunset over the Carpathian Mountains and thinking of you. We'll get back to our sunset-watching spot at home soon. Let me know how the book is going. Love from Mike." They stamped a forget-me-not on the last page of each letter, after their signatures.

"What is with these forget-me-nots?" exclaimed the neurological team at St. Michael's Hospital. "Plastic, silk, fresh, drawings, photos, even tattoos—they all trigger release of the most soothing and relaxing hormones. They calm you just by looking at them. Touching the flower petals has an even more powerful effect. Patients with Alzheimer's disease and any other memory impairment are showing remarkable improvement."

Many personal electronics makers collapsed after the confirmation of MLS Syndrome, as people began to shun their tablets and smartphones. Other developers rose to the challenge, building hardcopy printers into the devices. Some engraved a forget-me-not on the device's shell. In just five years after the report, educators and psychologists announced improved concentration on tasks by children and adults, less forgetfulness, and a greater sense of commitment to loved ones and family. Traffic fatalities dropped as distracted driving behaviours and road rage disappeared. Daily life became less frustrating and more enjoyable everywhere.

Carol Shetler is occasionally a writer, but mostly an editor. She edited The Future is Short: Science Fiction in a Flash, Volume 2 *in 2015. Most recently she has edited a collection of 200-word short stories for a client. One of her client's books,* Wrath of an Angry God, *was nominated for a 2016 Dragon Award in the military SF category. When not editing, Carol loves to read military and alternative history SF, mysteries, and biographies. She keeps fit with weight training and figure skating. With her best friend, she also watches several classic movies on DVD every week.*

END OF THE WORLD

December 2016

Winner
"Rearranging Worlds"
Jack McDaniel

Rearranging Worlds

Jack McDaniel

What does a puddle jumper know about the universe?

Lilith sucked in air, held her breath, squatted, and jumped for all she was worth. A few feet later she landed—SPLASH!—two-footed in a small puddle. She giggled.

The rain had finally abated two hours earlier and stopped completely just an hour ago. The sun and the equatorial latitude of the island conspired to dry up the puddles along the walkway within minutes, the baking sun trying to claim back that which had fallen for the previous two days. The Gods who giveth also taketh away.

"You are a silly child," Peter grinned.

She grabbed his hand, sucked in air, jumped again. SPLASH!

"'course I am. I'm nine."

They walked down the hill towards the beach. For days she had been telling him with certainty that she was leaving and that she couldn't come back. He was baffled, shocked. They were a team, the old man and the young girl. She couldn't just leave. Where would she go?

They had found each other a couple of years ago. She was wet and scraggily as if she had just crawled from the sea, an orphan. He was lonely, misplaced, and counting days as if there were meaning in their number. He had taken her home with him, like a stray cat found along the roadside. They had struggled together for a while but eventually found balance. And he found something he had lost—purpose. How the world had changed.

There was no way to make him understand. So she was patient. In due time, she had said a couple of days ago, you will understand.

"If I were in charge of the world, I would have it rain every morning."

"Why?" Asked Peter.

"Puddles are whole worlds. They fall from the sky one drop at a time. Every drop that falls or trickles in adds a new dimension to that world. Morning rain means lots of new things and new worlds created."

"But, based on your actions today, you destroy worlds."

Lilith squeezed his hand and smiled.

Peter stopped and looked at her. The world is ending, he thought, and she giggles while jumping from one puddle to the next. In his anger and frustration at her announcement, he hated her—her nonchalance, her care-free attitude, her innocence. And he loved her for it, wished he could co-opt it, make it his own. But he couldn't. He had responsibility now. He had duty. There were expectations. He was, in a manner of speaking, a parent. Good Lord! He felt the weight of all of it and it owned him.

"I destroy nothing. I just re-arrange things. They all get sucked back up to the sky eventually, anyway. Just so they can fall again and create more new worlds, new possibilities."

"The rain," she continued, with a smirk and haughty attitude, "only knows that it must fall. It has no intent. It seeks no path." She was mocking him and his teachings. "But on the ground, well, that is another matter. Raindrops form puddles, congregate together, and await the jumps of little girls, and the chance to fall again. Play and discovery and experience is what they are about."

"Humph."

Peter stopped. He stared ahead, unblinking. They were at the end of the road. Others from town were standing along the beach and lining the pier, those brave enough and not in denial, anyway. Sadie the grocer was there, crying. "This is the end of the world," her voice loud and clear.

Others joined in. "It is!", "Hear dat", "Too true, Sadie"—trying to convince themselves of the truth before them, heads nodding, mumbling.

Hovering over the water in front of them was a ship. Just hovering, a whisper of a hum from its anti-gravity engines. It had a slick white surface, no visible windows. The side opened and a walkway extended to the pier.

"So, this is it," Peter shook his head, dismayed. "Stupid orphan."

"This is it, angry old man."

They laughed at their inside joke.

"You going to the stars in that?"

Lilith smiled. "That puddle-jumper? No. The big ship is up there. In space."

Peter scratched his head. "I think I understand."

They said their goodbyes. Peter ignored the questions of the crowd of people. On the walk home there were a couple of puddles still remaining from the previous days' rains. He jumped towards one of them, landed two footed—SPLASH! He laughed out loud. Another world, he thought, rearranged.

Jack McDaniel is a writer, artist, and graphic/web designer who lives in Colorado, USA. His essays and short fiction have appeared in various places on the web and in print, including: Storybook, Tiny Lights Literary Journal, *and* Technorati. *You can learn more about him at www.agentsoftheundertow.com.*

BETWEEN A ROCK AND A SOFT PLACE

J. J. Alleson

Stranded aliens seek earth's prime location.

"The Brightstars say they need more space."

My sister Kris always could pick the moment. This one was right on the Double Edge, with an excellent view across the sheer expanse of glass. From there we observed both the buffoons of officialdom in their pandering grey livery, and the drifting white wisps in the sky below.

There was only one place we could be: the World Welcoming Committee's Bi-annual Convention on the 128th floor of Melbourne's Eureka Tower. My emerald space-tutu and I flounced over to where platters of fauxroo steaks and redeye cheesecake sat tersely beside more exotic delicacies. Half-way through downing a flute of 4X champagne, I pointed vertically.

"Plenty up there."

I made for a very non-scientific, unsympathetic confidante. Some of you may remember five years ago when WWC managed to FUBAR First Contact with Venus. By some evolutionary miracle, life had evolved on that viciously hostile planet in one barely hospitable area: its atmosphere. But when WWC gave out the contracts for reception pods, they thought it best to ignore the suggestions of a renowned biochemist: Kris.

As a result of their cost-cutting, 26 amorphous arrivals, aka Brightstars, were sucked out of containment by Earth's . . . 10% extra gravity or something. Nine days later, the Starship *'Disgusted of Venus'* departed, leaving its fellow aliens lost among our clouds. Rumour was they'd preferred the much gentler kiss of Earth's atmospheric pressure. Anyway, the whole fiasco had created a new buzz-term: 'friendly leakage'.

Now Kris plucked the champagne from my hand and finished it off. "They want to negotiate for the Pacific."

"Quelle surprise."

Venusians were fascinated by water. Those fogs rolling across Earth's lakes and oceans weren't home-made anymore. Those were the Brightstars, seeking *location, location, location.* Still, our marine life was healthy and thriving. Balanced desalination and the removal of toxic elements would be the bung for this property transaction.

"They've had to dive in at the hostile end of evolution, Kira. They're supreme in adaptation; in survival. They've even taken on human features to reassure us."

"I'll give you they no longer sound like rusty foghorns," I said. "And as far as I can tell, they haven't body-snatched any of us in our sleep. Yet."

Right on cue, a gentle voice came from behind to offer us galactic harmony. "Hi, Kris, Kira. You're looking beautiful tonight."

I turned in very slow motion. "Hello, CK. As are you."

Clark Kent was a Brightstar who'd taken on a very smart Earth name. With hilarious irony, he was now also a member of WWC. Tonight, he was manifesting a vintage tuxedo with a smoky look that might have seemed sexy to some weakened minds.

"Kira, I will see you next week at Leran's London exhibition?"

"You will indeed, Clark."

After more pleasantries aimed directly at me, Clark drifted off. Stiff with indignation, I turned back to Kris. "Does it seem right that on *our* planet they're superheroes and on theirs we become a smackdown?"

Smackdown was another buzz-term popularised by various eateries. It was a thin pancake made from some unidentifiable matter that had been pulped, then flattened, then baked to a crisp. Initially savoury, they'd become very sweet. Secretly I was convinced restaurants had done this to help alleviate any bitterness at having being twinned with a horror like Venus.

Kris smiled at me encouragingly. "Clark likes you. And tests show they're adjusting without artifice. Becoming truly more humanoid."

"Uh-oh."

I didn't have Kris's technical mind. My skills lay in being quick on the very ominous uptake—or as others might mutter, paranoid. Still, even I could retain a few scientific nuggets. The Venusians reproduced faster. They were quicker, sparklier, and more flexible. They could fly.

And a base population of 26 simply wasn't enough.

"Would it be the end of the world, Kira?" My sister's eyes suddenly seemed extra shiny under my gaze.

"As we know it? *Yes.*"

I thought about humans still in thrall to legendary vampires, werewolves, and long-leggedy beasties. Now we had aliens who also happened to be superheroes.

Five years ago, ditties about acid rain had been easy. And rhymes about love were a doddle. I just hoped that matching that earthly emotion with the term 'interplanetary' would mean nothing more for Earth's future than a brief war of words.

J.J. Alleson is a multi-genre freelance writer based in London. An avid observer of human nature and behaviour, she writes non-provincial science fiction that extrapolates and reflects all sections and groups of human society. She has published a number of short stories as well as nonfiction pieces. She is currently working on a humourous romance guide, Her Cheekbones were so Pointy, *due to be published on Amazon. In her other work she is a business consultant and community advocate. In her spare time, she enjoys London life and culture.*

FINAL SHIP TO MARS

Helen Doran-Wu

A family's desperate attempt to leave Earth on the final ship to Mars.

I strapped Toby into his chair. I tested the straps and smiled in his face. He had been silent for two days now. Shock. I kissed him brusquely on the cheek, my stubble rasping on his soft skin. I looked at Jean. She just stared at Toby. Her mouth was pinched. Her tear stains were a grim reminder of what she, we, had left behind. Guiltily, I could not help but feel relieved despite everything. Knowing this was the end. Knowing that we may have left it too late but we were leaving.

I sat down and strapped myself in. No pleasant hostess explained the routine. No warm towels or juice and a charming smile. No laughter from holiday makers bustling with bags and souvenirs. This was the last ship leaving Earth. Most silently prayed that gravity would not pull us back onto the launch pad and into the crowds below. Into the ones being left behind. And then, suddenly, the engines roared with the deafening thunder of burning fuel.

Shuddering, the chair lurched forward, thrusting me against the straps. Burning, aching muscles clenched in my jaw, my back, up into my head. My tooth cracked with a sharp stabbing pain. Pulsing throbs pounded in my eyes. I was helpless to do anything but surrender to the pilots and the pain.

Sweat ran down my arms dripping onto the floor. I watched helplessly as a puddle formed on the deck. Its fluid shuddering and vibrating in rhythm with the roaring engines. The sound of power pounding through flesh and fluid. Nausea rose up from my lurching stomach. Vomit, acrid and violent, hurtled through the air. I closed my eyes in shame.

Dimly through the stink, I grew aware of Jean's leg crammed against mine. Slowly and carefully, turning my head I tried to see her more clearly. Her ashen face was drawn tight. She stared ahead. Her eyes fixed on nothing. Thin unyielding lips refusing to scream. Refusing to acknowledge the horror. I noticed her blood-smeared shoe. She had kicked a woman hard in the face. The woman had tumbled off the stairs, too stunned to even screech. Grabbing Toby's arm, Jean had desperately pulled his small body through the wall of heaving flesh and onto the ship. But that woman would be dead. If not today, then in the final phase. She had killed a doomed woman and saved our son. I tried to squeeze her hand, to feel her warmth. But her taut fingers gripped the chair. A cold and clammy sweat clung to her skin.

The ship's engines thrust hard in a desperate fight against gravity. For a brief second the ship hung in the air, laden with people, fear and hope. And then it lifted, pushing Earth's dying arms away. Our ship, the final ship, was on its way to Mars.

Helen Doran-Wu is a writer from Western Australia. She loves nothing more than to hide in the dark cool of her bedroom and write.

THE COLLECTIVE

Chris Nance

When the world ends, do we accept the help of our alien saviors?

"You have to eat, Mr. Anderson," my wife said. "After all, we'll need you healthy if you're to join The Collective. This is the fifth meal in a row that you've declined."

Maybe it was the low blood sugar talking but I really wasn't in the mood for a debate. So I pushed the plate away. "I'm not eating your stinkin' food," I replied, and meant it. I didn't want anything to do with their attempts to domesticate me. They lied to us and we were too desperate.

It was about a decade ago that the moon exploded. An asteroid, they said, plunged through its core, shattering it. Tremendous chunks showered the Earth while the bulk of the lunar debris drifted off into space. We never saw it coming: a "random act of God," our best scientists claimed. Still, we were so sure of ourselves . . . so sure of our own technology . . . of our ability to adapt to even the worst disaster. We were wrong.

The fallout was more than just the impact effects creating a nuclear winter; the ocean's tides almost completely stopped and the finely balanced environments of the Earth plunged into chaos. Whole species and ecosystems disappeared in a mass extinction. We began running out of food. Without the sun, sea currents, and tides, the microorganisms of the oceans disappeared . . . along with the fish, insects, and other animals that depended on them, including us. Mankind was devastated and only the strongest survived. Broken and desperate, we looked for a miracle.

So you can imagine that The Collective was a gift from Heaven. Their ship appeared out of nowhere, offering rescue for our species that seemed too good to be true. Their community of worlds brought hope; here were dozens of races from around the galaxy, content and with a collected purpose. At least that's what they claimed . . . and we went willingly.

They told us there would be hard work, but there was more than enough for all. They were at least honest in that regard, but there's an old expression that says "sometimes the answers you receive depend on the questions you ask." We never thought to ask if there was a price.

After ten years of scrounging from old food stores and sickly plants, most every man, woman, and child was more than ready, so we left for space. The aliens were more than eager to give. Truthfully, we were provided ample food and witnessed wonders few of us could ever imagine. In retrospect, we were less dubious than we probably should have been.

We reached their Collective as refugees within just a few weeks. They explained that it would take time to process all of us, of course. After all, integrating millions of immigrants took time, they claimed, and there were over four hundred groups in front of mine. My wife's was forty-seventh. The day her group was called was the last time I saw her, because what came back was not my wife . . . at least not the woman I loved. Sure, she looked the same, but the mechanical tone in her speech and her emotionless expression told the truth. It was as if her fondness for me was erased and replaced by something too analytical, too well designed. She'd been rewritten.

I heard a few of the processed, the reprogrammed humans, talking the other day. They were like my wife, emotionless drones. Robotically, they evaluated their new assignments in the nearby asteroid field. One of them made the mistake of providing too much detail, talking without uncertainty about their weapon, an Asteroid Rail Gun.

They were so proud of it; you see? We'd been set up to fail from the beginning. The aliens destroyed our moon and sold us on the promise of a new beginning. They waited patiently for our world to die, until only the strongest were left, until we were desperate . . . because they can only take control if you're willing. And they needed more workers. More slaves.

"Number four hundred seventeen," they announced.

"Your number's up, Mr. Anderson," my wife explained coldly.

"In more ways than you know," I replied. "What if I refuse?"

"You'll have that option, of course." She smiled mechanically. "I'm pleased to say that, so far, we've had 63 percent compliance."

"And the other 37 percent?"

"They did not comply."

"Will it hurt?" I asked. I'd never known them to lie, so I'd consider her answer sincere.

"Only if you don't comply," she responded.

So I enjoyed my last meal.

For the last decade, Chris Nance has been helping people improve their health, in his busy chiropractic office in Arizona, but his real passion has always been more creative. Specifically, he's a huge science fiction fan. So far, he has completed several scifi and fantasy manuscripts geared toward the middle grade, young adult, and adult markets and he is in the process of securing an agent to represent those works. Also a talented artist, Chris is currently working on the artwork for two children's fantasy books he authored. When not spending time with his wife and three kids or running his office, he can be found writing or painting. Chris also enjoys exploring the mountains of Arizona and traveling, when he has the opportunity.

LIFEBOAT XX-3

Ben Boyd, Jr.

Escaping from one world may not mean escaping.

The sleek, needle-nose designed XX-3 spaceship continued toward the light beyond the gray barrier. The once perfect world, poisoned by uncontrolled population growth, in two months became a mutilated battleground of misery and death. Three concurrent years of extreme air pollution turned the toxicity levels in the atmosphere to lethal. The life or death battle for clean air erupted into global warfare. The XX-3 became the only option to survive.

"My Dearest, it is inevitable. We can talk all day, but the facts will not change. We are doomed unless we can penetrate the outer barrier." Captain Dario Eonix, pilot and scientist, whispered softly to his lovely wife, Lieutenant Mavis Eonix, the navigation engineer, as they lay in bed in the Captain's cabin at dawn on the third day of their desperate mission.

"I am very afraid, Dari. We are deep into the unknown. The XX-3 is unproven. It has never faced these challenges. Our thick atmosphere adds so much pressure and resistance. The structural design may fail. If we survive the break through, what then? Nobody knows what lies beyond. I fear our ship will not withstand these challenges."

"What are our other options, my Love?" The XX-3, designed to carry fifty carefully selected pairs of people, carried the last hope of continuing the species.

"Captain Eonix, please report to the bridge." The screaming wrist radio spoiled what might be their last few moments of intimacy.

"We have to go to work," Mavis announced as she pulled on her robe. "Unless we had twenty minutes more . . ."

"Stop teasing me, you beautiful temptress. I am still the Captain of this ship and duty calls," he laughed.

"Sir, I also address the Captain of my heart." She smiled sadly as she realized this moment might never come again. Her mind drifted back to her husband's argument with Admiral Thadie, Fleet Commander. She beamed with pride when Dari refused to end the experiment. He told the Admiral a new world could be found. He demanded the Admiral consider the quantum physics theory everyone studied at the Academy. Dari pleaded for the Admiral to believe other worlds and forces existed beyond the barrier. Mavis smiled as she watched Dari put on his uniform.

"You are right, my love. I am that Captain also." He chattered. "However, I need to answer my summons. Join me on the bridge in an hour if you wish or I will meet you in the galley for coffee later." He kissed her passionately, possibly for the last time.

"Lieutenant Harden, what have you got," Eonix asked.

"Sir, we are encountering strange phenomena. The closer we move towards the barrier the more light we see. Sometimes we see great bursts of light which only last a second or two.

"Look there! See what I mean." The light flashed brilliantly, but ended quickly.

"I don't know what to make of it. Any other changes when this occurs?"

"Yes, the electrical systems seem to stop for a moment with each flash and we are experiencing a gradual increase in temperature the closer we come to the barrier."

"Strange indeed. The higher temperatures were foreseen. The light flashes were not. What does our Flight Engineer think about this? I did not see any such red flag notes," the Captain demanded.

"The Operations Engineer said negative on the flashes and if the rate of temperature change continues to increase, it will critically affect the inside of this spaceship until we reach the barrier."

"Interesting Lieutenant. How critical and exactly when will we be at the barrier?"

"We will be at the barrier in exactly two hours and forty-nine minutes. The temperature will be extreme. Pressurized suits will be required, Sir."

"Order it done, Lieutenant."

The sleek spacecraft burst through the top of the teardrop shaped barrier. The crew shouted their cheers of happiness having escaped their doomed world. The spaceship immediately doubled its speed turning the crew's exuberance into terror in seconds as another barrier appeared almost instantly. A blinding light erupted then disappeared.

"Captain! Look! Another barrier just like the one we left is dead ahead. We're going to crash! We are moving too fast! We'll all die! God help us!"

Seconds before impact, a hole appeared in the barrier. The tiny spaceship disappeared inside. A tube of light blazed a path. Moments later a green and blue ball appeared at the end of the light path.

The Singularity lowered His hand and smiled.

Ben Boyd, Jr. is a freelance science fiction/fantasy/action/adventure author, screen writer, and self-publisher who lives with his wife in the Great Smoky Mountain foothills near Maryville, TN. His four-novel series, **The Fall of the Americas,** *is available on Amazon including book five,* **Seven Paths to Higher Ground,** *released in April 2016. He is a member of the Writers' Workshop of Maryville, Knoxville Screenwriters Group, and the Knoxville Writers' Guild. When not writing, he and his wife grow organic vegetables, and brew fruit wine.*
Website: www.benboydjr.com; Contact: bhboyd2012@gmail.com, on Facebook https://www.facebook.com/ben.boyd.5030 or on Twitter: https://twitter.com/BenBoyd24

Acknowledgement

Writing Science Fiction is usually a lonely endeavor; however, thanks to Jot Russell, the *Science Fiction Microstory Contest* Group (on Goodreads and formerly on LinkedIn) offers the opportunity for like-minded writers and readers to engage in a vibrant, diverse, worldwide community. With intriguing monthly themes and thoughtful critiques, the group's expertise and wide-ranging viewpoints supports, encourages, and elevates each writer to create some of the best stories they have ever written.

Bringing these stories together in an anthology is no small task. For their efforts, we fervently applaud the editors: Paula Friedman, J. J. Alleson, and Emily Johnson who have spent hours ensuring each story achieves its greatest effect.

Lillicat Publishers, a staunch supporter of writers and always by our side, artfully solidifies this diverse selection of stories into this riveting anthology.

If you are a lonely SF writer or avid SF reader, please visit the group on Goodreads and experience the power of a thriving writing community.

S. M. Kraftchak
Editor and Compilation Director

READ
THE FUTURE IS SHORT
SCIENCE FICTION IN A FLASH
VOLUME 2

READ
THE FUTURE IS SHORT
SCIENCE FICTION IN A FLASH
VOLUME 1

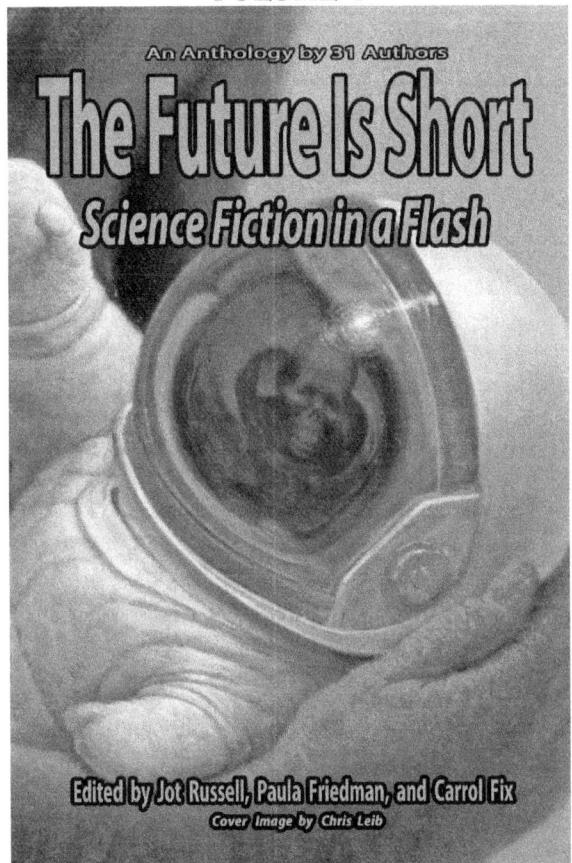

An Anthology by 31 Authors

The Future Is Short
Science Fiction in a Flash

Edited by Jot Russell, Paula Friedman, and Carrol Fix

Cover Image by Chris Leib

Visions VI
Galaxies

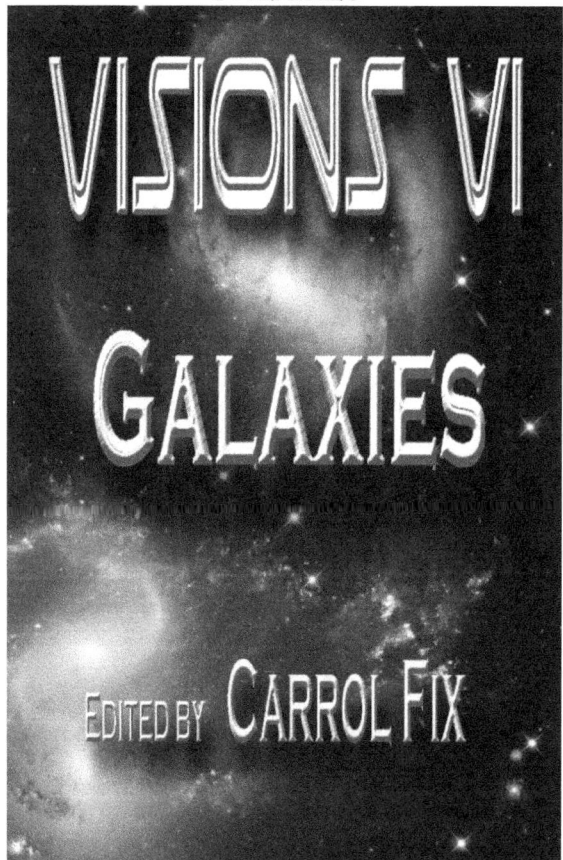

VISIONS V
MILKY WAY

EDITED BY CARROL FIX

EDITED BY CARROL FIX

VISIONS III
INSIDE THE KUIPER BELT

VISIONS II
MOONS OF SATURN

VISIONS
LEAVING EARTH

. . . and coming soon!

THE FUTURE IS SHORT
SCIENCE FICTION IN A FLASH
VOLUME 4

AND

VISIONS VII: UNIVERSE

www.ingramcontent.com/pod-product-compliance
Lightning Source LLC
Chambersburg PA
CBHW070812180626
46818CB00001B/228